Dear Parents:

Congratulations! Your child is taking the first steps on an exciting journey. The destination? Independent reading!

STEP INTO READING® will help your child get there. The program offers five steps to reading success. Each step includes fun stories and colorful art or photographs. In addition to original fiction and books with favorite characters, there are Step into Reading Non-Fiction Readers, Phonics Readers and Boxed Sets, Sticker Readers, and Comic Readers—a complete literacy program with something to interest every child.

Learning to Read, Step by Step!

Ready to Read   Preschool–Kindergarten
• big type and easy words • rhyme and rhythm • picture clues
For children who know the alphabet and are eager to begin reading

Reading wi
• basic vocabu   ies
For children   d sound out
new words w

Reading on Your Own   Grades 1–3
• engaging characters • easy-to-follow plots • popular topics
For children who are ready to read on their own.

Reading Paragraphs   Grades 2–3
• challenging vocabulary • short paragraphs • exciting stories
For newly independent readers who read simple sentences with confidence.

Ready for Chapters   Grades 2–4
• chapters • longer paragraphs • full-color art
For children who want to take the plunge into chapter books but still like colorful pictures.

STEP INTO READING® is designed to give every child a successful reading experience. The grade levels are only guides; children will progress through the steps at their own speed, developing confidence in their reading.

Remember, a lifetime love of reading starts with a single step!

WE ARE THE JUSTICE LEAGUE!

Published in the United States by Random House Children's Books, a division
of Penguin Random House LLC, 1745 Broadway, New York, NY 10019, and in
Canada by Penguin Random House Canada Limited, Toronto. The works in
this collection were originally published separately as *Batman: I Am Batman,*
copyright © 2016 DC Comics; *Wonder Woman: I Am Wonder Woman,*
copyright © 2010 DC Comics; *Superman: I Am Superman,* copyright © 2009
DC Comics; *Justice League: I Am The Flash,* copyright © 2014 DC Comics;
Justice League: I Am Aquaman, copyright © 2013 DC Comics.

Step into Reading, Random House, and the Random House colophon are
registered trademarks of Penguin Random House LLC.

Visit us on the Web!
StepIntoReading.com
rhcbooks.com

Educators and librarians, for a variety of teaching tools, visit us at
RHTeachersLibrarians.com

ISBN 978-0-593-12356-0 (trade) — ISBN 978-0-593-12357-7 (ebook)

MANUFACTURED IN CHINA
10 9 8 7 6 5 4 3 2 1

WE ARE THE JUSTICE LEAGUE!

Step 3 Books

A Collection of Five Early Readers

Random House New York

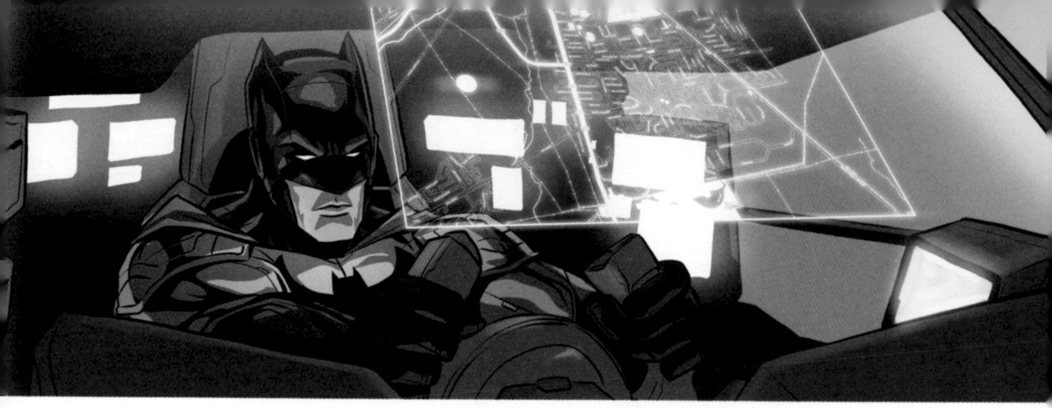

CONTENTS

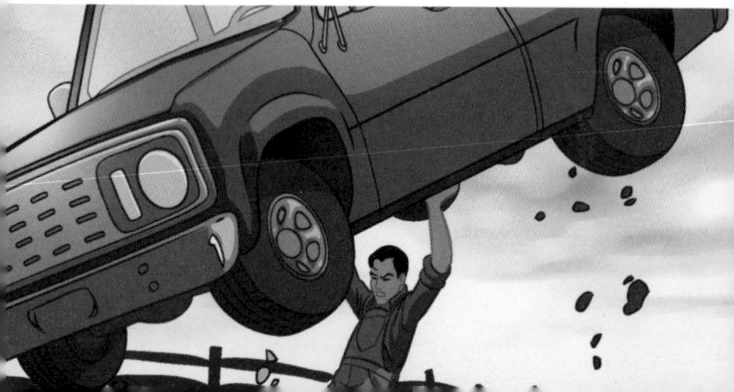

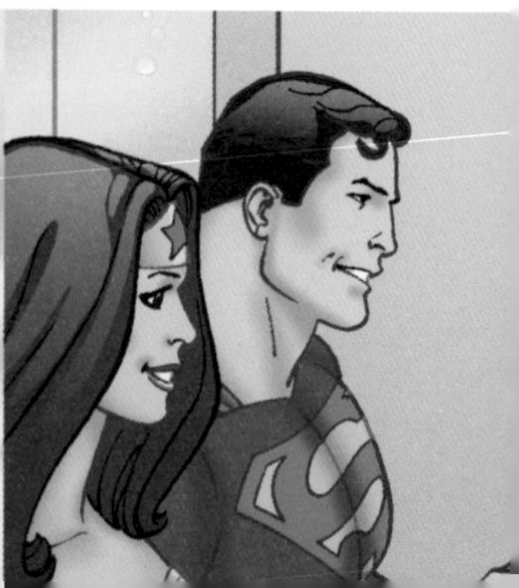

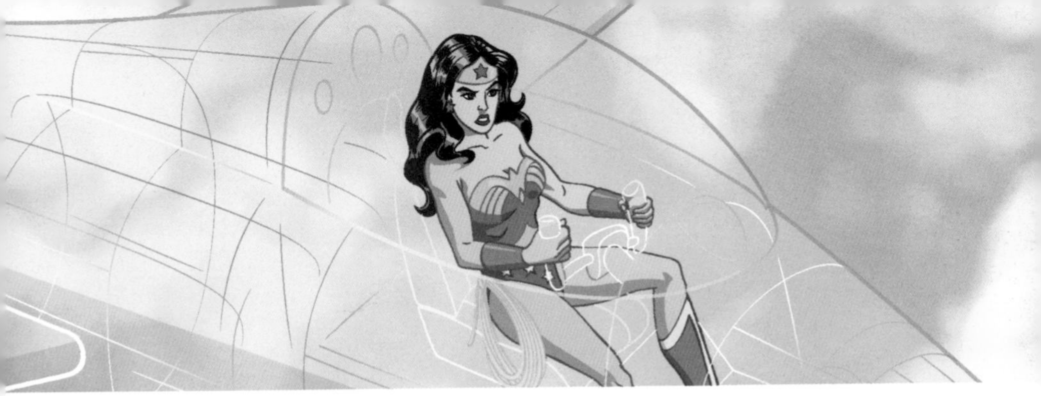

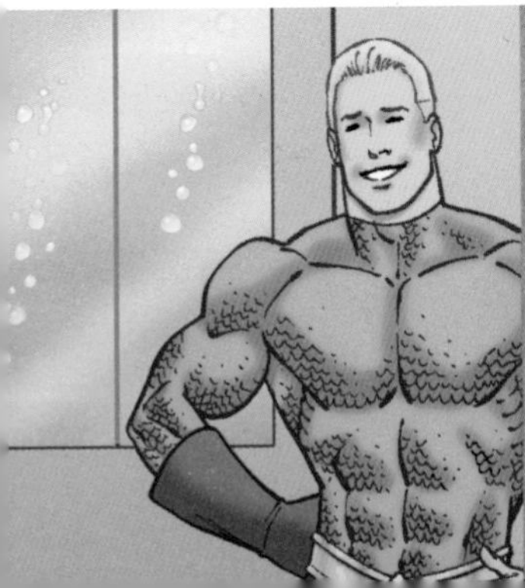

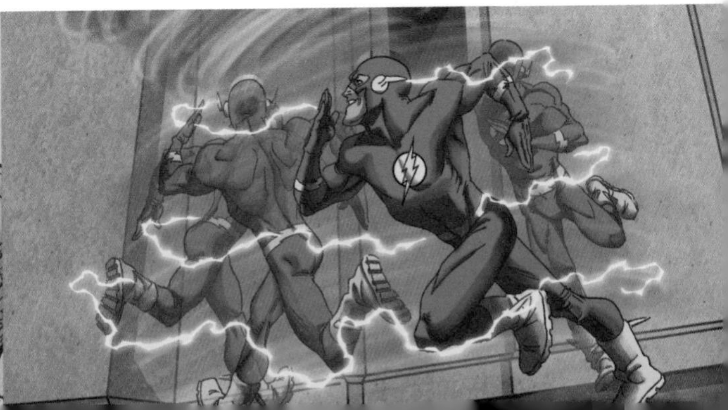

BATMAN ™

I AM BATMAN

based on a story by Delphine Finnegan

illustrated by Andie Tong

Batman created by Bob Kane with Bill Finger

Random House 🏠 New York

My name is Bruce Wayne.

I live in Gotham City.

I own Wayne Industries.

We build big planes, small computers,
and other high-tech gear.

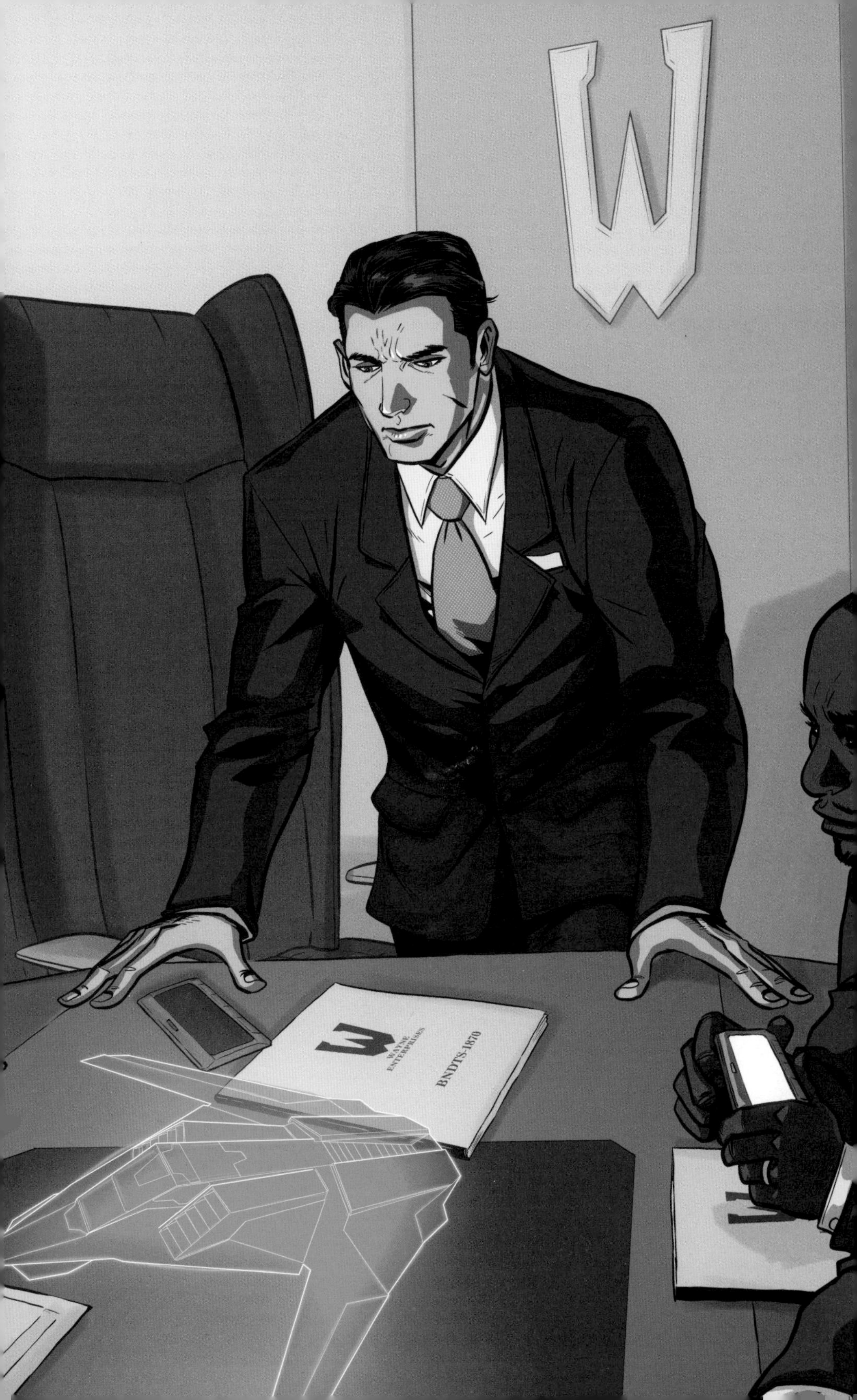
WAYNE
ENTERPRISES
BNDTS-1870

I use my technology
to make phones better
and cars faster.

When I get home,
I head to a secret cave
and change into my
super hero outfit.

I am Batman.

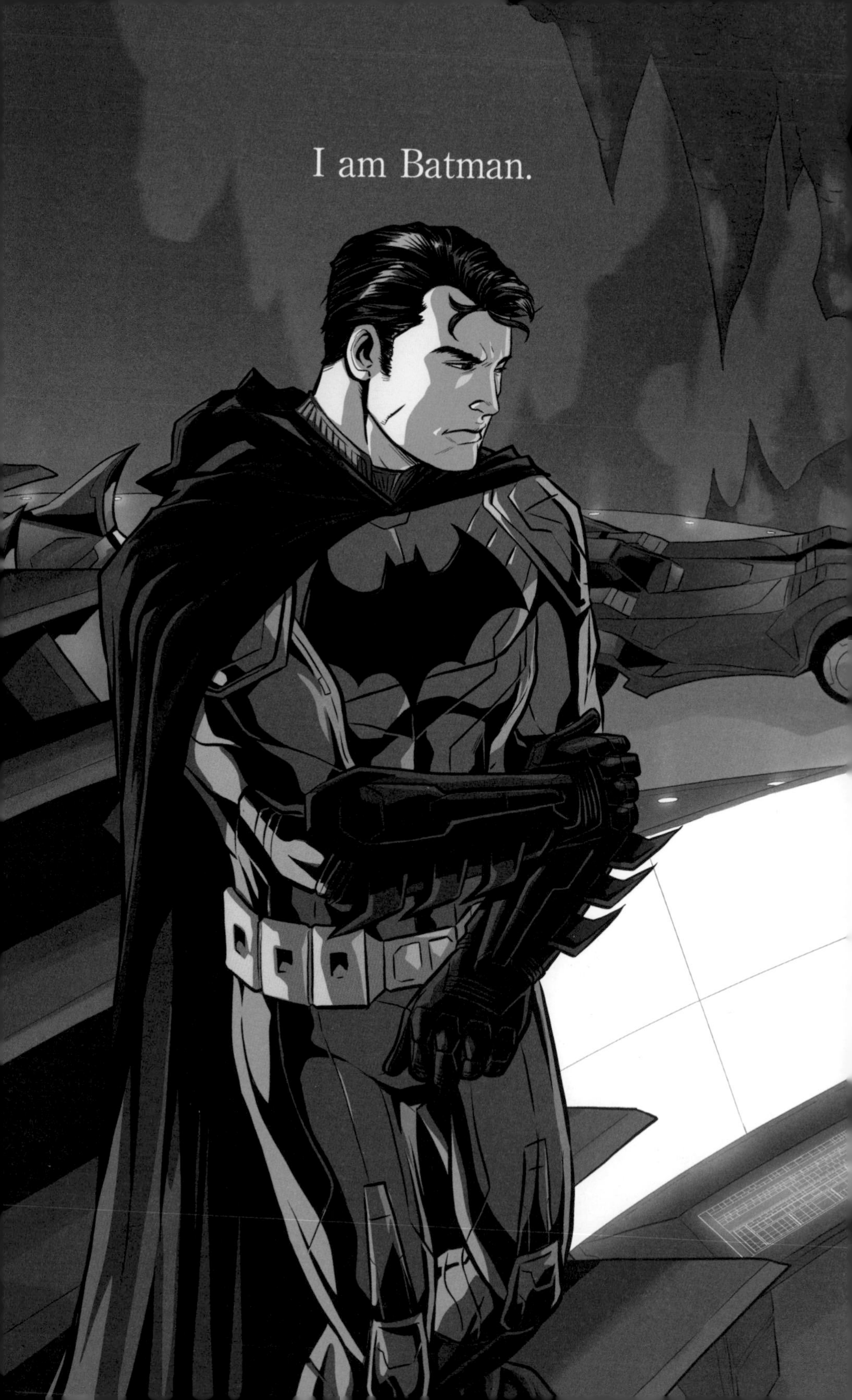

I protect Gotham City.
Alfred is my butler.
He helps keep
my identity a secret.

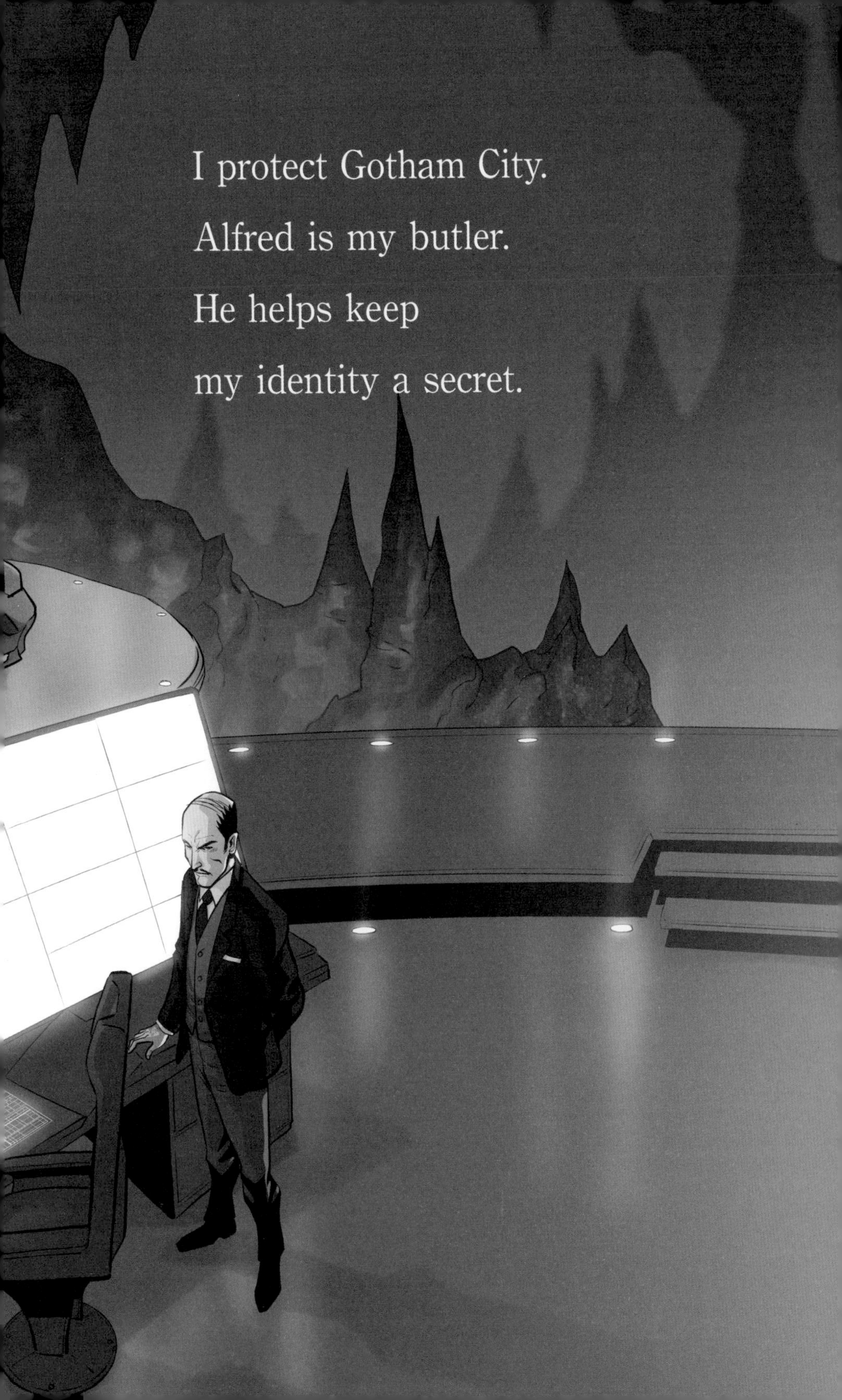

Alfred spots the Bat-Signal.

Someone needs my help!

I put on my mask.

I check my Utility Belt.

Now I am ready!

I jump into the Batmobile.

It is a super-fast car!

I call Commissioner Gordon.

He is in charge of the police.

He sends me to

the Gotham City Museum.

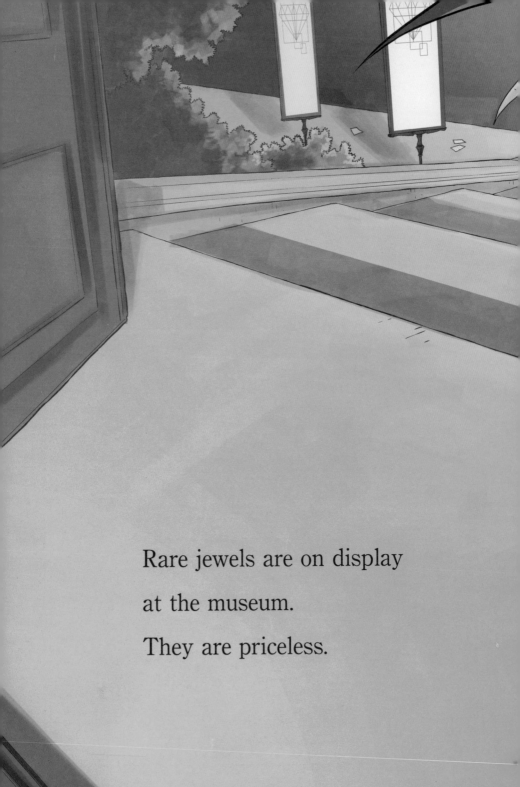

Rare jewels are on display
at the museum.
They are priceless.

But the guards are gone!

The doors are wide open,

and the alarm is broken.

I find the guards tied up

in the main hall.

Suddenly, a net falls over me.

I am trapped by
Catwoman, the Joker,
and the Riddler!

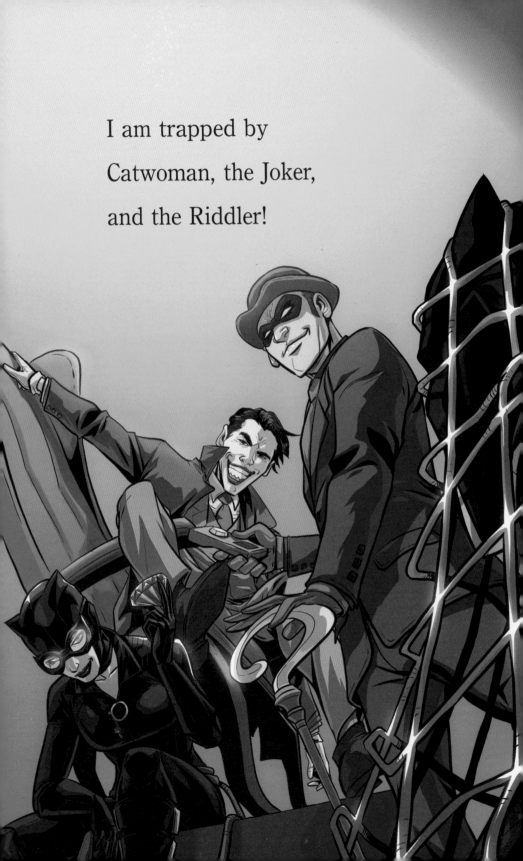

I twist and turn.

I try to escape

while the thieves

pack their bags.

My Batarangs are sharp.

I use them to cut the net!

I act fast to catch the Riddler.
But the Joker and Catwoman
get away.

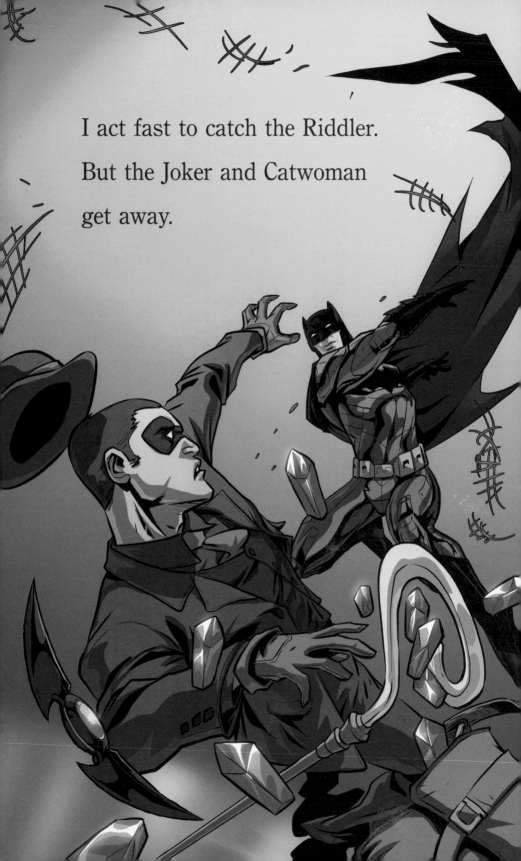

I leave the guards to handle the Riddler while I look for the other villains.

The Joker hops into
a helicopter.
Catwoman runs
the other way.

I toss a tracer

at the helicopter.

It is a direct hit!

Then I follow Catwoman.

She runs fast and far!

But I do not give up.

I chase her until

there is nowhere left to go.

That makes two villains down
and one more to capture.
I check the tracer.
The Joker is hiding nearby!

I hop into the Batmobile
and race off to find
the Joker and the
missing jewels.

The Joker is relaxing

in his hilltop hideaway.

He shares stolen loot

with his crew.

I wait for the right time to strike.

The villains are surprised!

I quickly tie up the crooks.

The Gotham City police arrive.

They take the bad guys to jail.

The jewels will be returned

to the museum.

When Gotham City needs my help,

I will always answer the call.

I am Batman!

WONDER WOMAN™

I AM WONDER WOMAN

based on a story by Erin K. Stein

illustrated by Rick Farley

Wonder Woman created by William Moulton Marston

Random House 🏠 New York

My name is Princess Diana.

I grew up in a secret place

called Paradise Island.

I am an Amazon.

Queen Hippolyta is my mother.
She rules the Amazons
and protects Paradise Island.
All Amazons are strong warriors.

The Greek gods warned my mother
about dangers in the world.
Humankind needed someone
to keep the world safe.

The gods wanted to send the best
Amazon warrior to do the job.

The queen held a contest to see
which of us was faster, stronger,
and braver than all the rest.

I was a princess, but I did not
want to become queen.
I wanted to fight for justice!
I secretly entered the contest.

I tried my best to win.

Every one of my arrows hit the target.

I outran all my Amazon sisters.

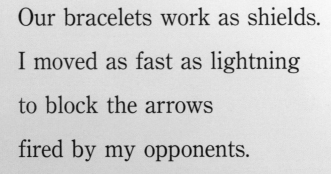

Our bracelets work as shields.

I moved as fast as lightning

to block the arrows

fired by my opponents.

In the last sword fight,

I beat everyone.

After I won, I showed my face

to the crowd.

My mother was surprised,

but she was also very proud.

I was the champion!

She gave me a special outfit
and a new title: Wonder Woman!

The Greek gods gave me

a magic lasso.

It makes people tell the truth.

No one can see where I go

when I fly in my Invisible Jet.

This helps me keep

Paradise Island a secret.

Now I live in Washington, D.C.
I use the name Diana Prince
for my secret identity.

I work for a top-secret agency.

Whenever there is trouble,

I find out about it first!

Two reports have come in.

An old bridge will collapse

when the next train comes.

And there is a crime at the zoo.

I quickly change

into my super hero outfit.

I rush to the rescue

as Wonder Woman!

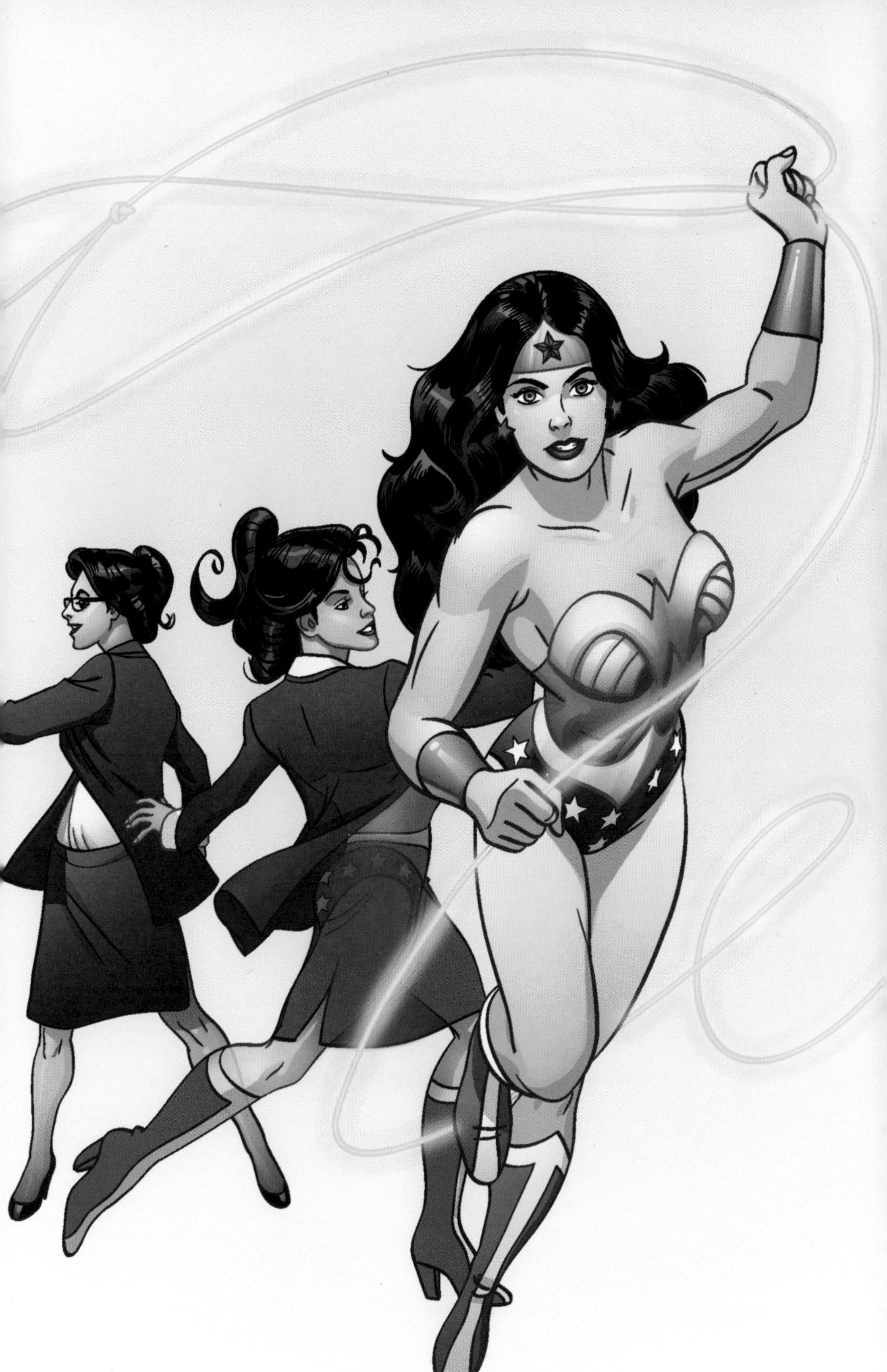

I fly through the city

faster than the speed of sound.

I use my super-strength

to help those in danger.

Just as the bridge collapses,

I carry the train to safety.

At the zoo, I find out

a tiger was stolen!

I use my Lasso of Truth

to catch the robbers.

The lasso makes them tell me

where they hid the tiger.

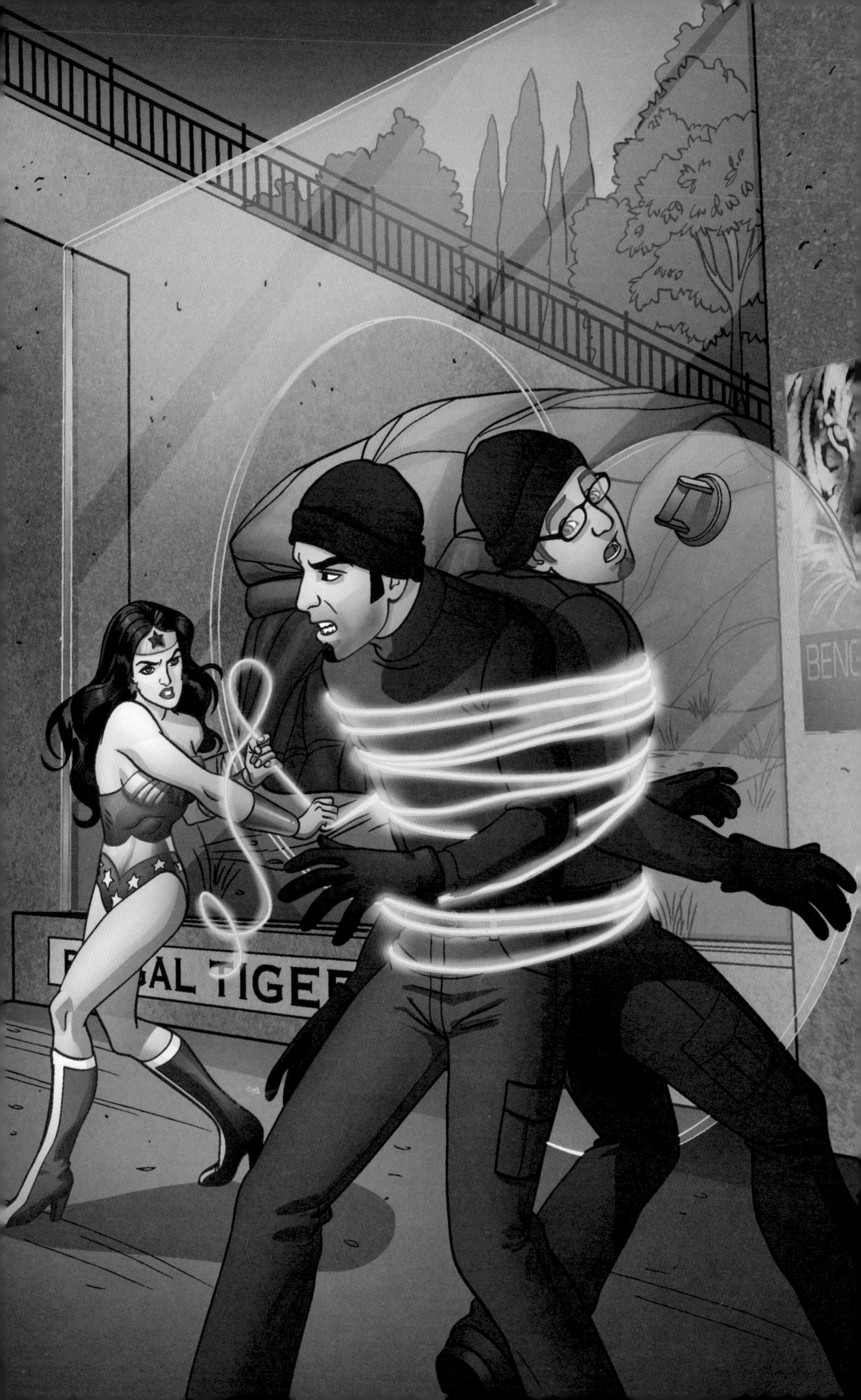
BENG
GAL TIGE

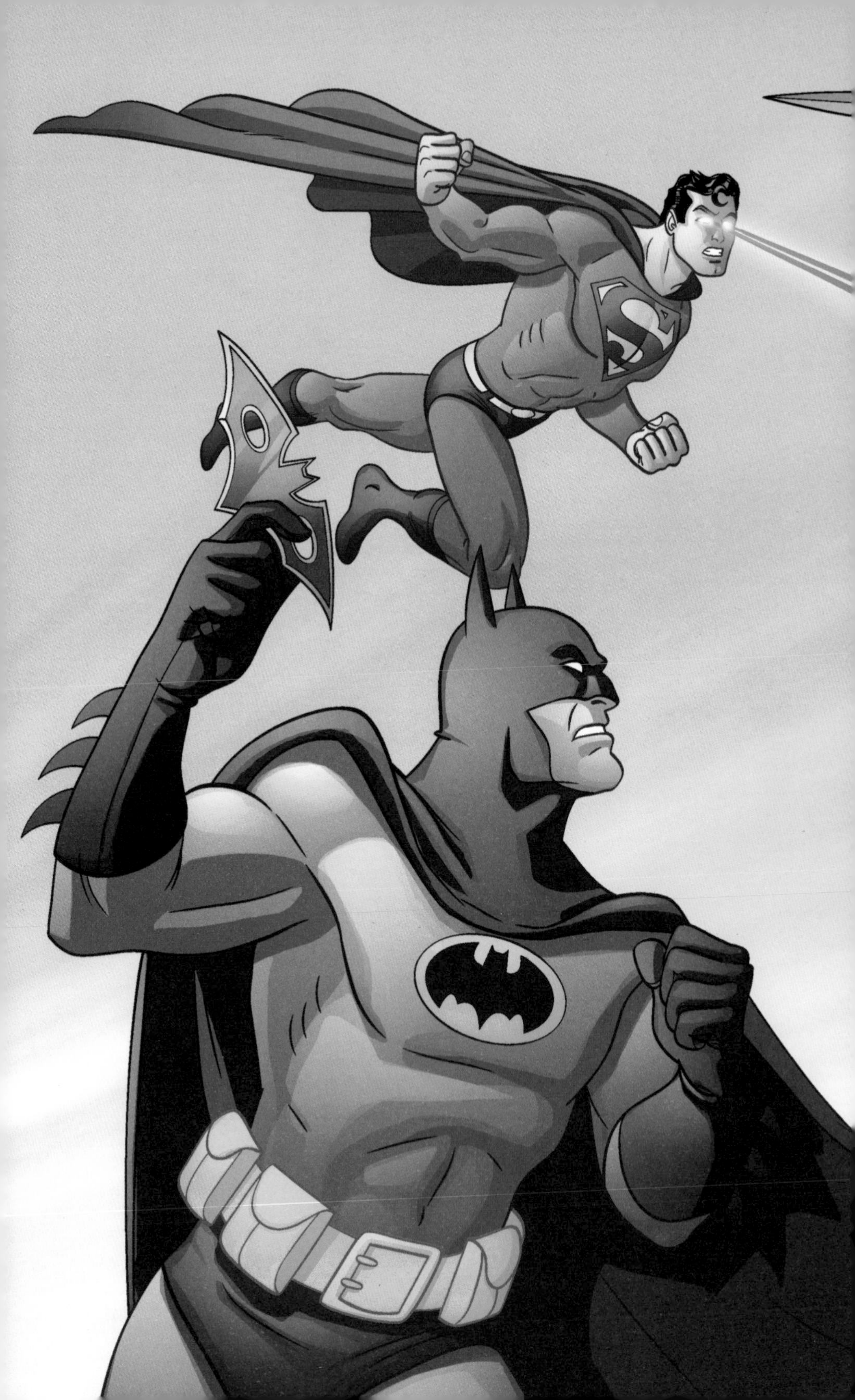

I have amazing friends.
Superman and Batman
help me train so I am never
caught off guard by my enemies.

We must be ready for anything,

even strange beasts!

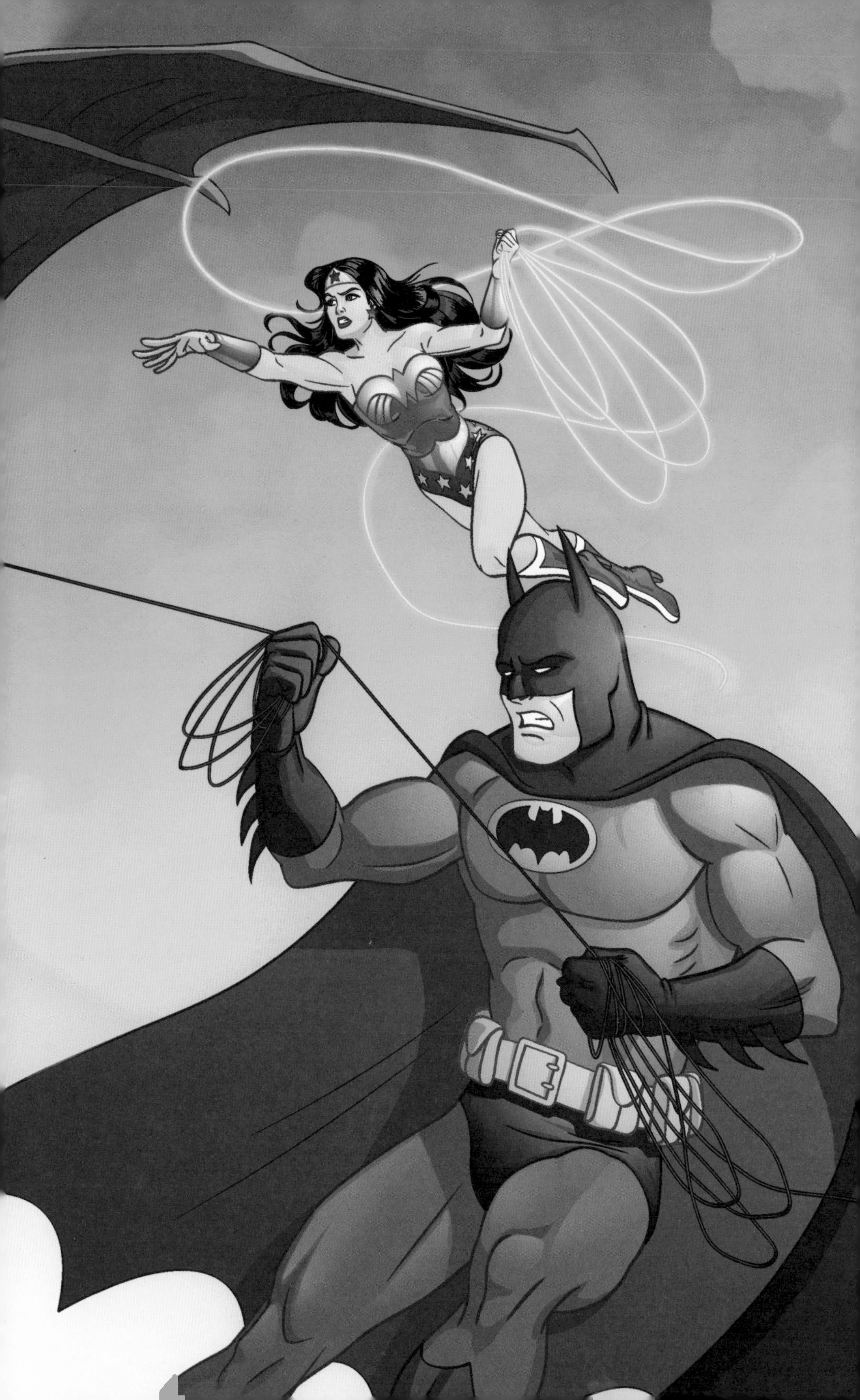

As Wonder Woman, I am famous.

But my secret identity

lets me live a normal life, too.

I am fast.

I am strong.

I am smart.

I am Wonder Woman!

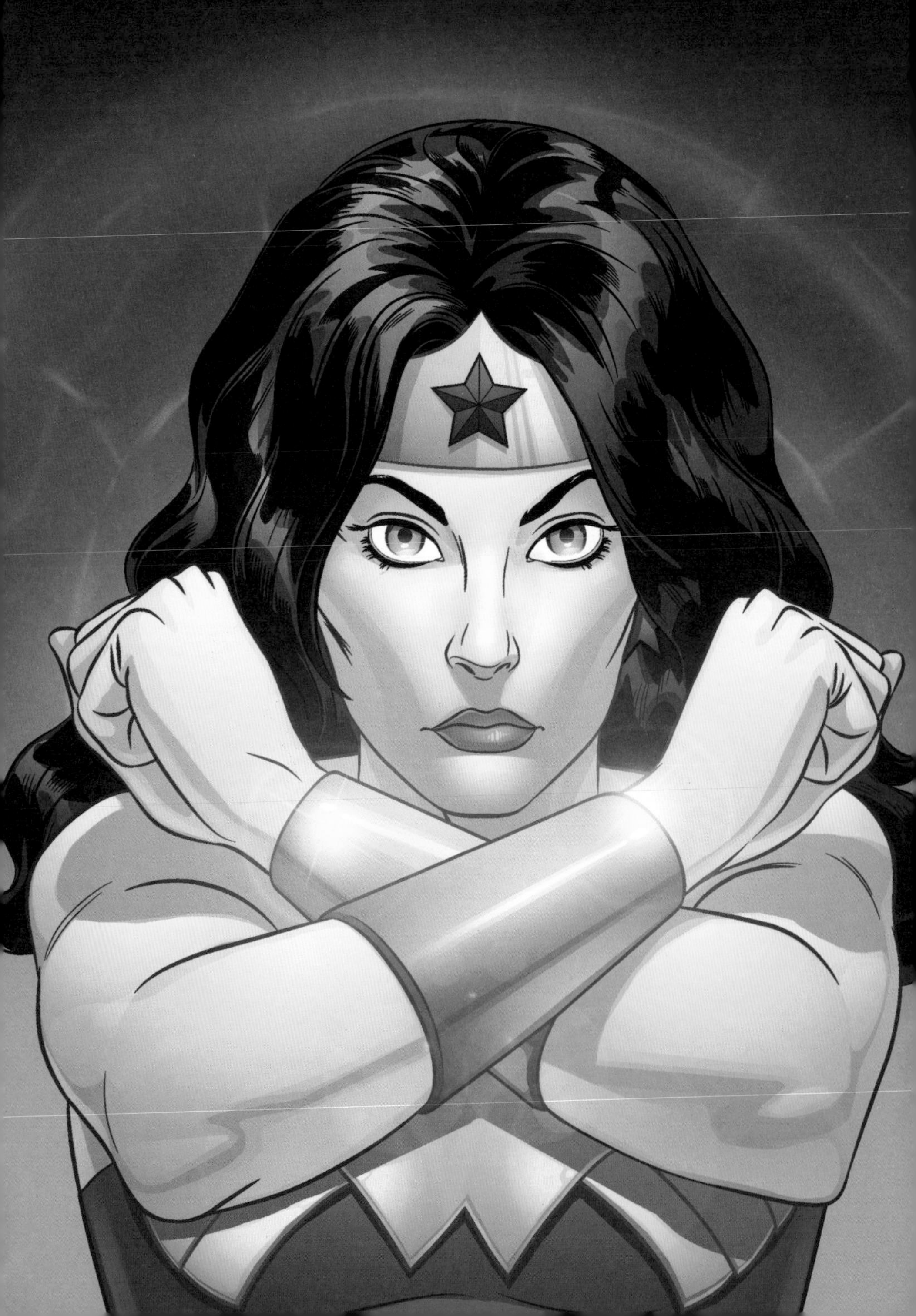

SUPERMAN

I AM SUPERMAN

based on a story by Michael Teitelbaum

illustrated by Rick Farley

Superman created by Jerry Siegel and Joe Shuster
By special arrangement with the Jerry Siegel family.

Random House 🏠 New York

My name is Clark Kent.

I am a reporter.

Lois Lane and I work

at the *Daily Planet*.

She races past me on her way
out of the newspaper office.
Lois is in a hurry,
so she must be working
on a secret story!

I know Lois is going to meet
Superman, so I change into
my super hero outfit. I rush
to the roof and see her.

I scoop her up when she arrives,
and off we go!

We are headed to the frozen Arctic.

To save time, I fly at super-speed.

I show Lois my secret home,
the Fortress of Solitude.

I use my super-strength
to lift a giant key, and
then I unlock the door.

To keep us warm, I use
my super-breath to blow
the door closed.

I show Lois the statues of my parents. My father's name was Jor-El, and my mother was Lara. The two statues are holding a model of Krypton above their heads.

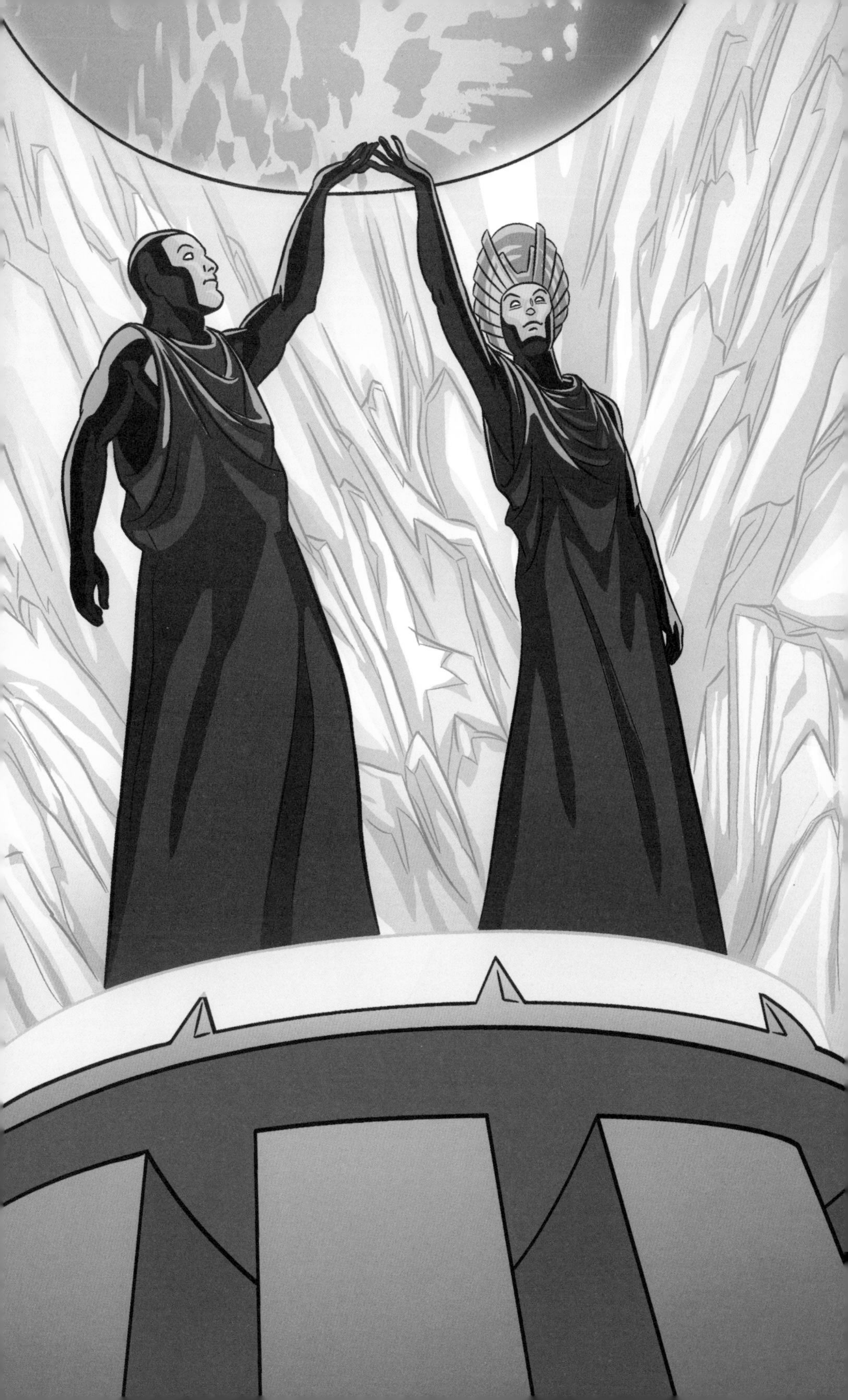

I pick up a special crystal and show Lois pictures of what life was like on Krypton.

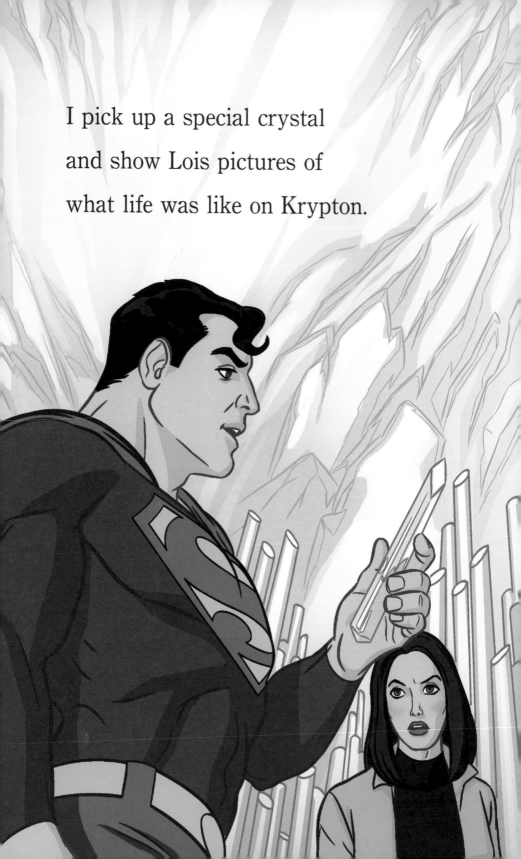

I tell her that Krypton

was different from Earth,

and it was my home.

One day, the planet exploded!

My father saved my life.
He put me in a spaceship
and sent me to Earth.

The yellow sun on Earth

gave me superpowers.

Even when I was a boy,

I could easily lift a truck!

Lois is amazed to learn
about my X-ray vision.
It allows me to see
through walls!

I tell Lois that although I am very strong, Kryptonite can make me weak. Kryptonite is actually a piece of my home planet. I keep it in a safe place so it cannot hurt me.

Suddenly, an alarm rings.

Lex Luthor is trying

to take over Metropolis!

I grab Lois and zoom out
of the fortress to stop him.

Just as we get back to
Metropolis, a building explodes.
I use my X-ray vision
to make sure no one is hurt.

Then I spot Lex Luthor
He is using a powerful laser
to cause the destruction!

As a wall starts to fall toward
Lois, I fly up and catch it.
I toss it safely away
from her.

Then I use my heat vision
to destroy the laser.
Lex Luthor is stunned!

He is also angry

that I stopped his evil plot.

The police arrive

and take him to jail.

Lois is excited because she has

an amazing story to write!

The next day, Lois hurries into my office. She tosses a copy of the *Daily Planet* on my desk.

The secret is out!

Her story about Superman

is front-page news!

I smile.

Lois does not know

there is more to the story.

I am Superman!

I AM THE FLASH™

based on a story by John Sazaklis

illustrated by Steven E. Gordon
and Eric A. Gordon

Random House 🏠 New York

I am Barry Allen.

I live in Central City.

I work as a scientist

for the Central City

Police Department.

But I am more than that. . . .

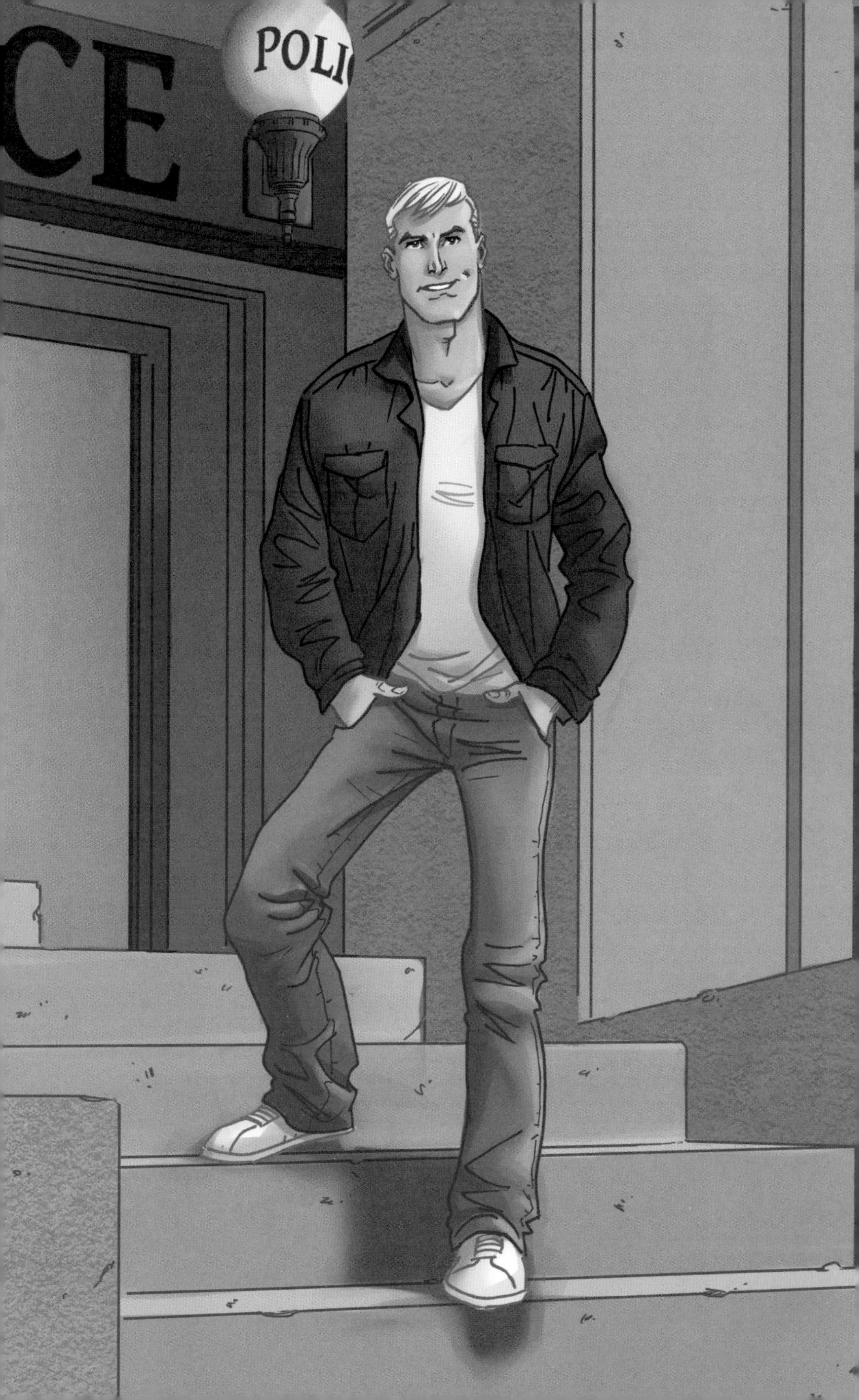
CE
POLI

A few years ago, I was working late in the police lab while a thunderstorm raged outside.

Suddenly, a bolt
of lightning crashed
through the window!

Many different chemicals from
the lab spilled onto my body.
The special combination
had a strange effect on me.

My body began to tremble
with incredible energy!
I suddenly felt the need to run!

I ran all the way home

in less than a minute.

The accident had given me

the power of super-speed!

I decided to protect

Central City with my new ability.

I created a special suit

to hide my true identity.

I became The Flash—

the Fastest Man Alive!

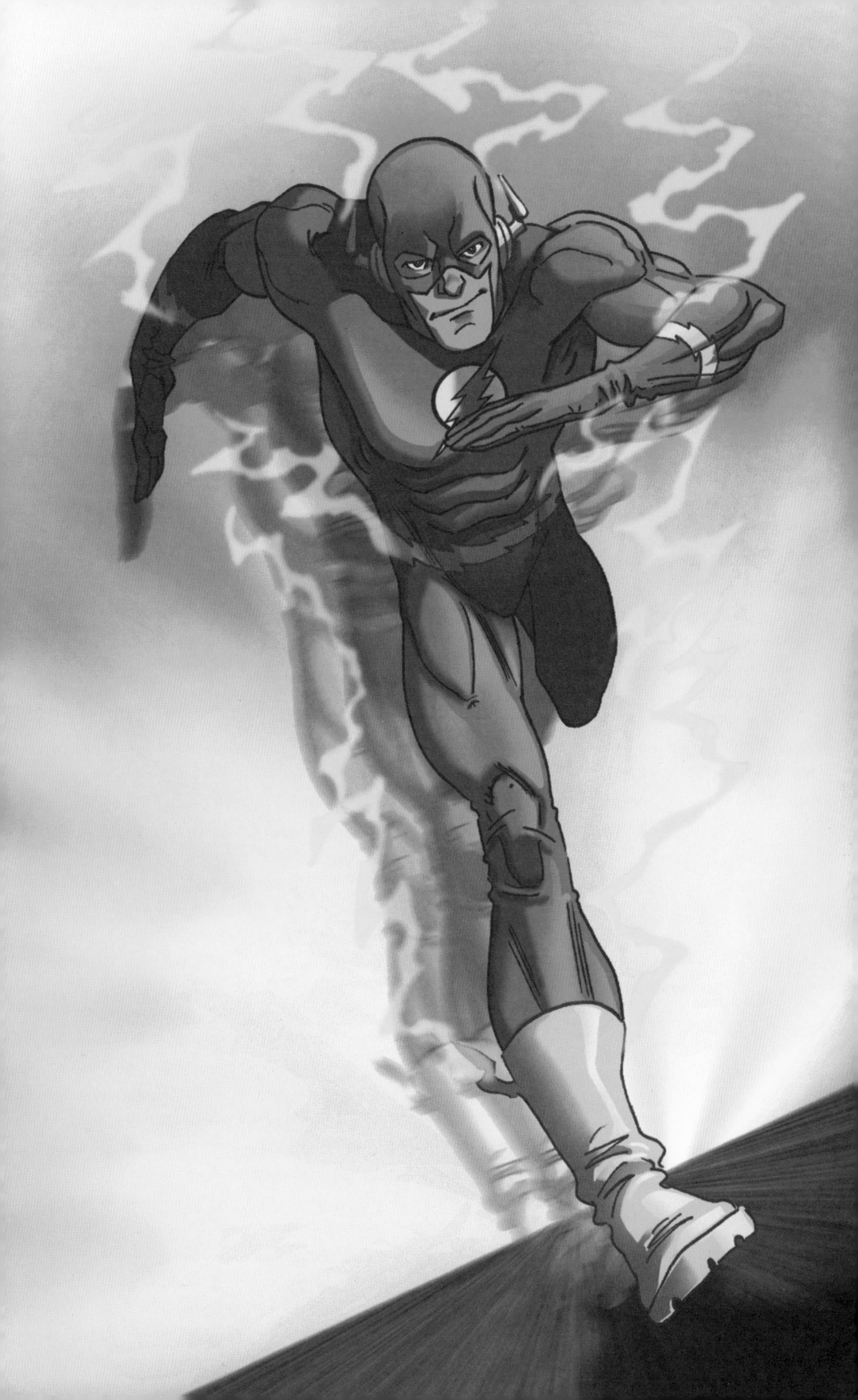

I fine-tuned my powers.

I could run up walls!

I could run on water!

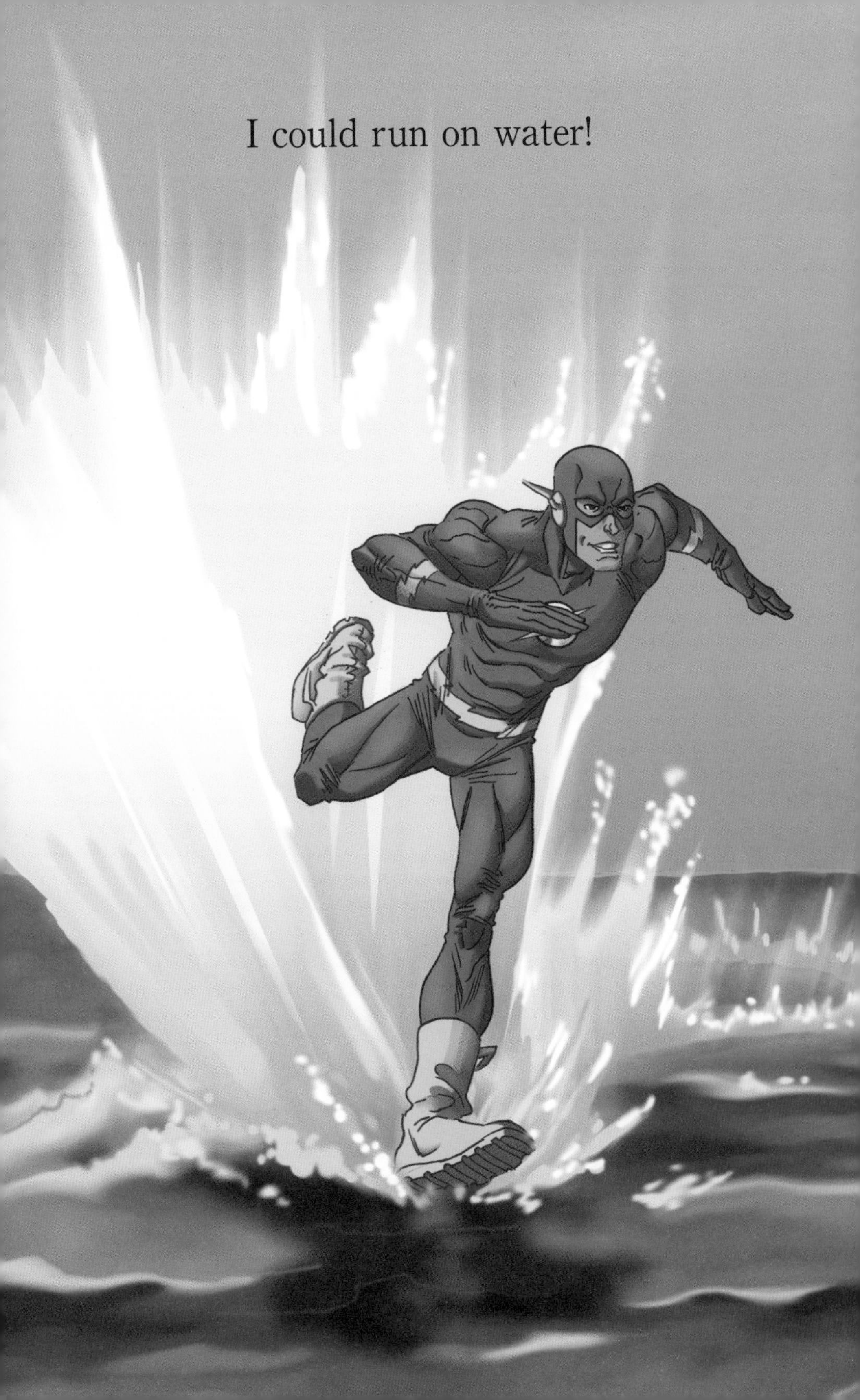

I could even create whirlwinds
by spinning my arms very quickly.

The crooks and criminals of
Central City were swiftly defeated
when I arrived on the scene!

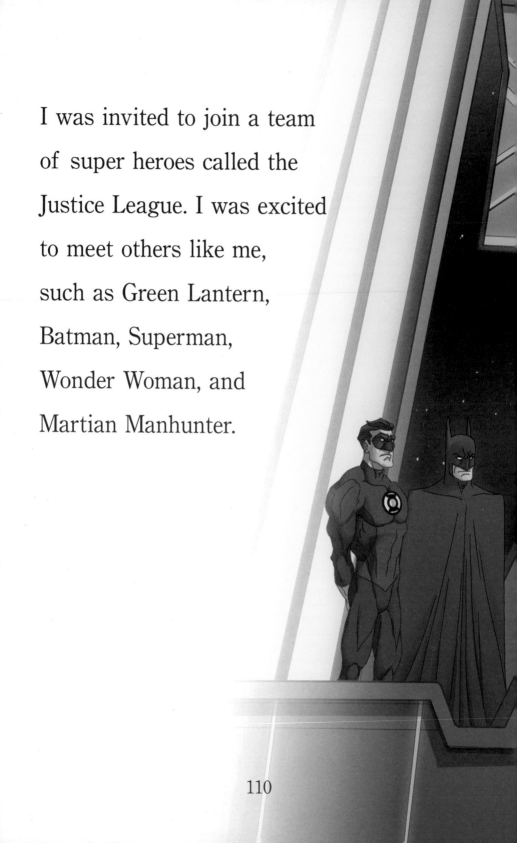

I was invited to join a team
of super heroes called the
Justice League. I was excited
to meet others like me,
such as Green Lantern,
Batman, Superman,
Wonder Woman, and
Martian Manhunter.

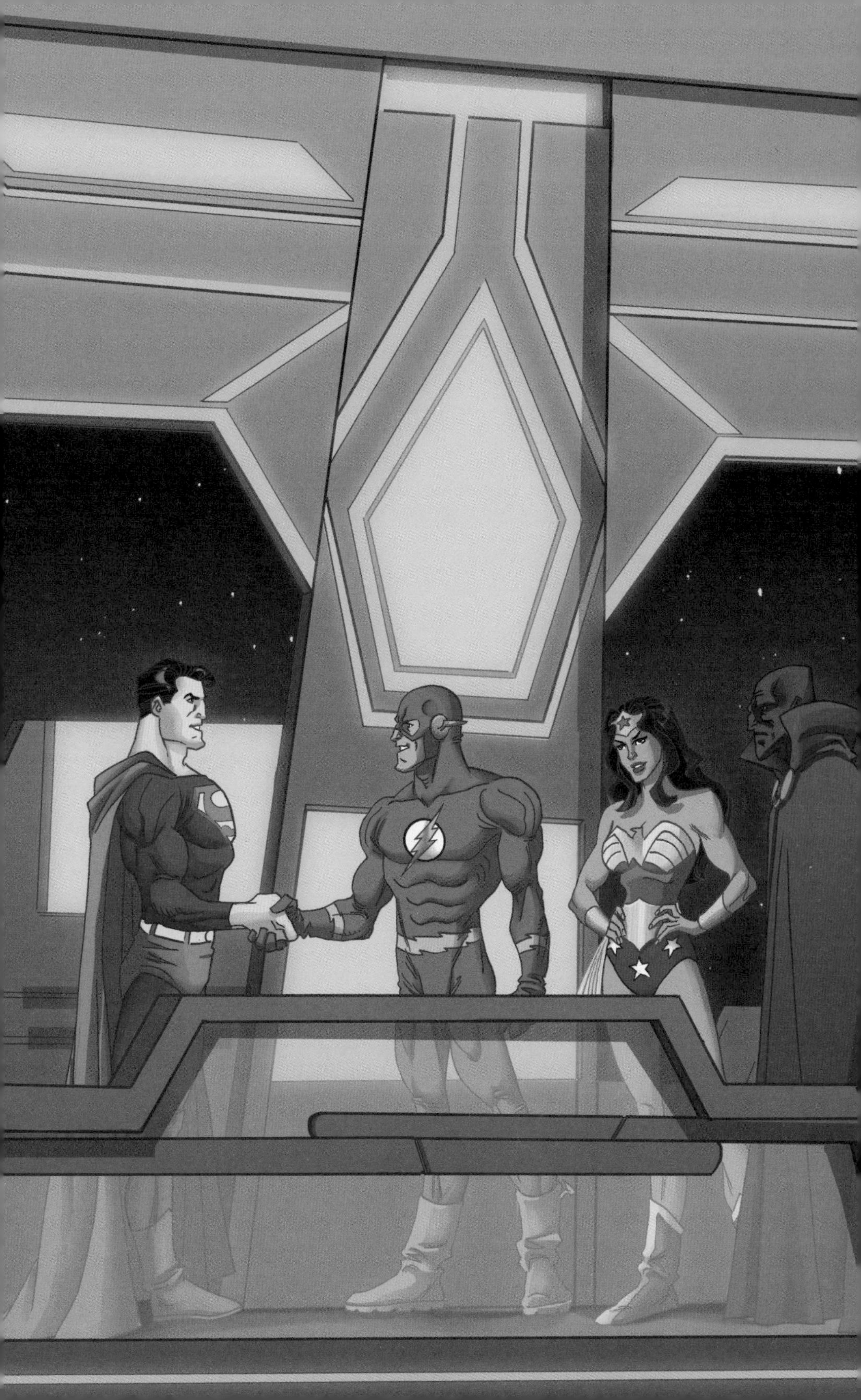

One day, I saw a news report on my television. A group of super-villains had broken out of jail!

In the blink of an eye, I became
The Flash and raced to the
scene of the crime!

On the way, I called
the Justice League for help.
When I arrived at the prison,
I spotted the mad scientist
known as Ultra-Humanite.

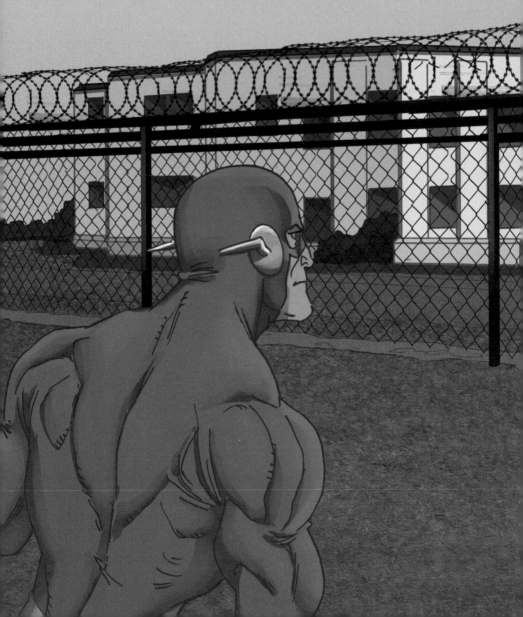

He had escaped alongside
the Weather Wizard, Captain Cold,
the Mirror Master, and
Captain Boomerang.

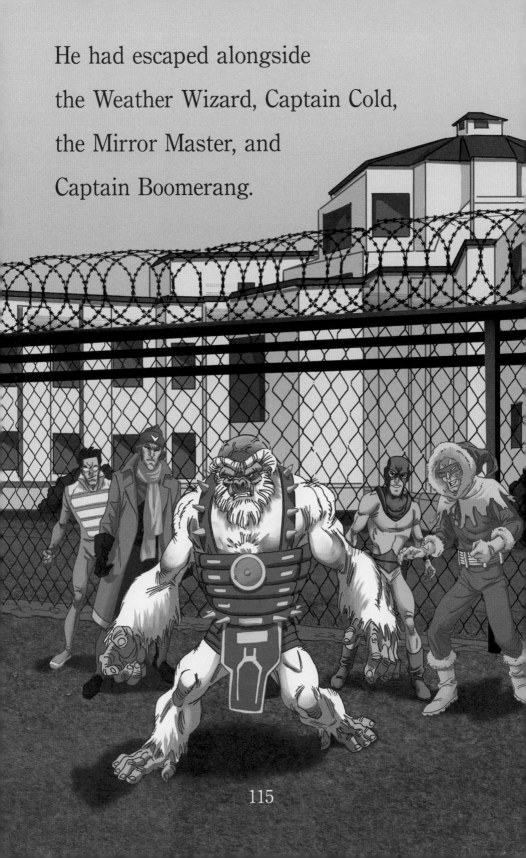

I kept the bad guys busy
until my friends arrived.

Before long, other members of the
Justice League arrived on the scene.
They are always ready for action!

Captain Cold tried to blast
Superman with his freeze ray,
but the Man of Steel put the crook
on ice with his freeze breath!

The Weather Wizard attacked
Batman with his weather wand.
But the Caped Crusader knocked
him out with a Batarang!

Captain Boomerang was
no match for Wonder Woman.
She easily tied him up with her
Golden Lasso of Truth!

The Mirror Master tried
to confuse Martian Manhunter,
but the hero used his mental powers
to take down the crafty crook.

Finally, I faced off
against Ultra-Humanite.
The mutant gorilla tried
to catch me,
but he was too slow!

I swiftly zigged and zagged

around the villain.

He never laid

a hairy hand on me!

I ran faster and faster in a big circle.

My speed created a tornado

that lifted all the villains into the air.

The strong winds sent the criminals

back over the prison wall—

where they belonged!

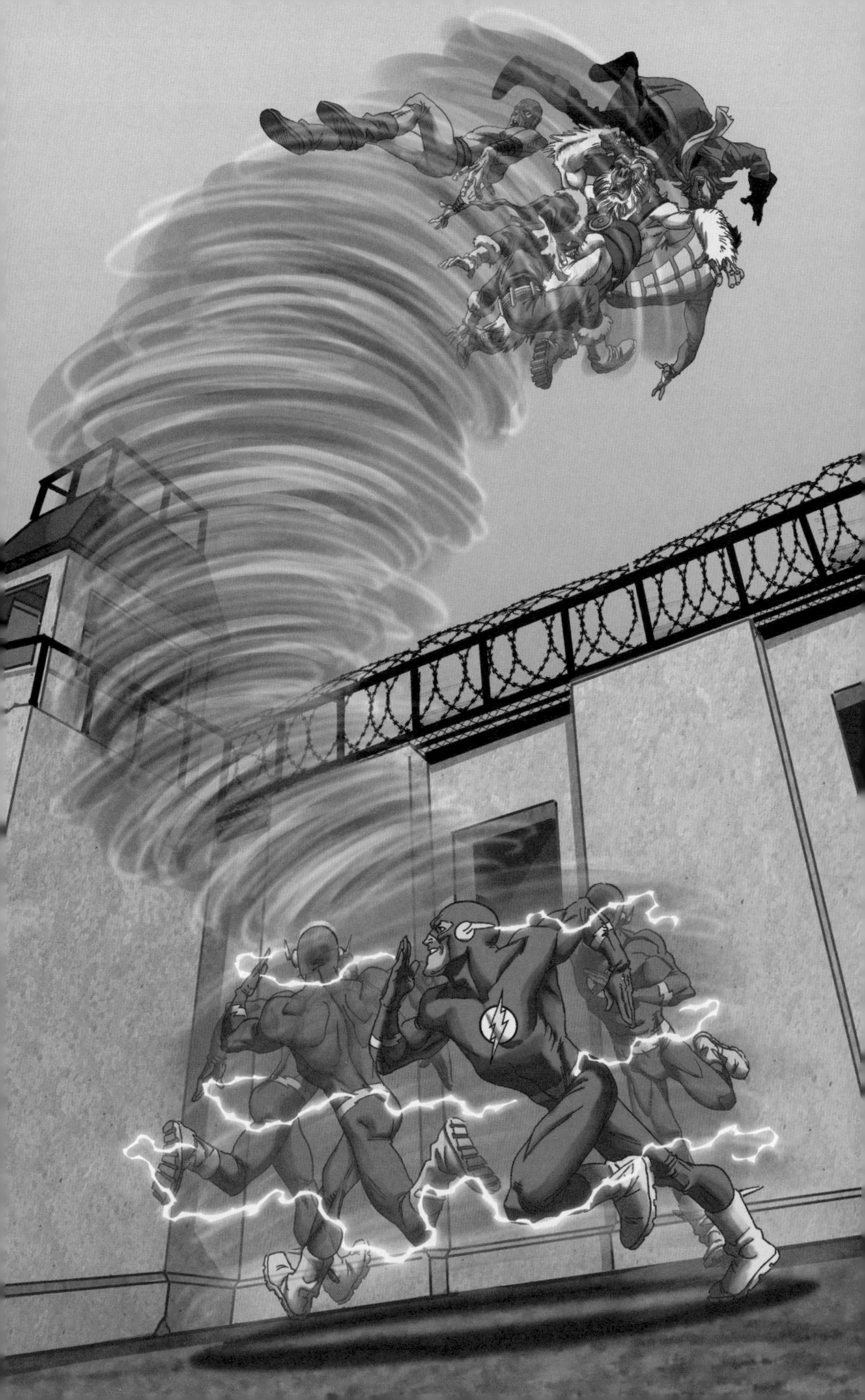

I am the protector of Central City.

I am the Fastest Man Alive.

I am The Flash!

STEP INTO READING®

I AM AQUAMAN™

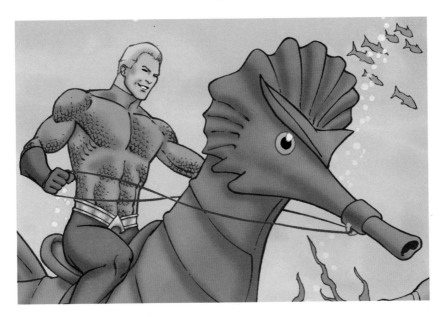

based on a story by Kirsten Mayer

illustrated by Andy Smith and Brad Vancata

Aquaman created by Paul Norris and Mort Weisinger

Random House 🏠 New York

The city of Atlantis

is under the sea.

I am Aquaman, King of Atlantis.

My wife, Mera, is the queen.

As a super hero, I protect the sea.

But I also help humans on land.

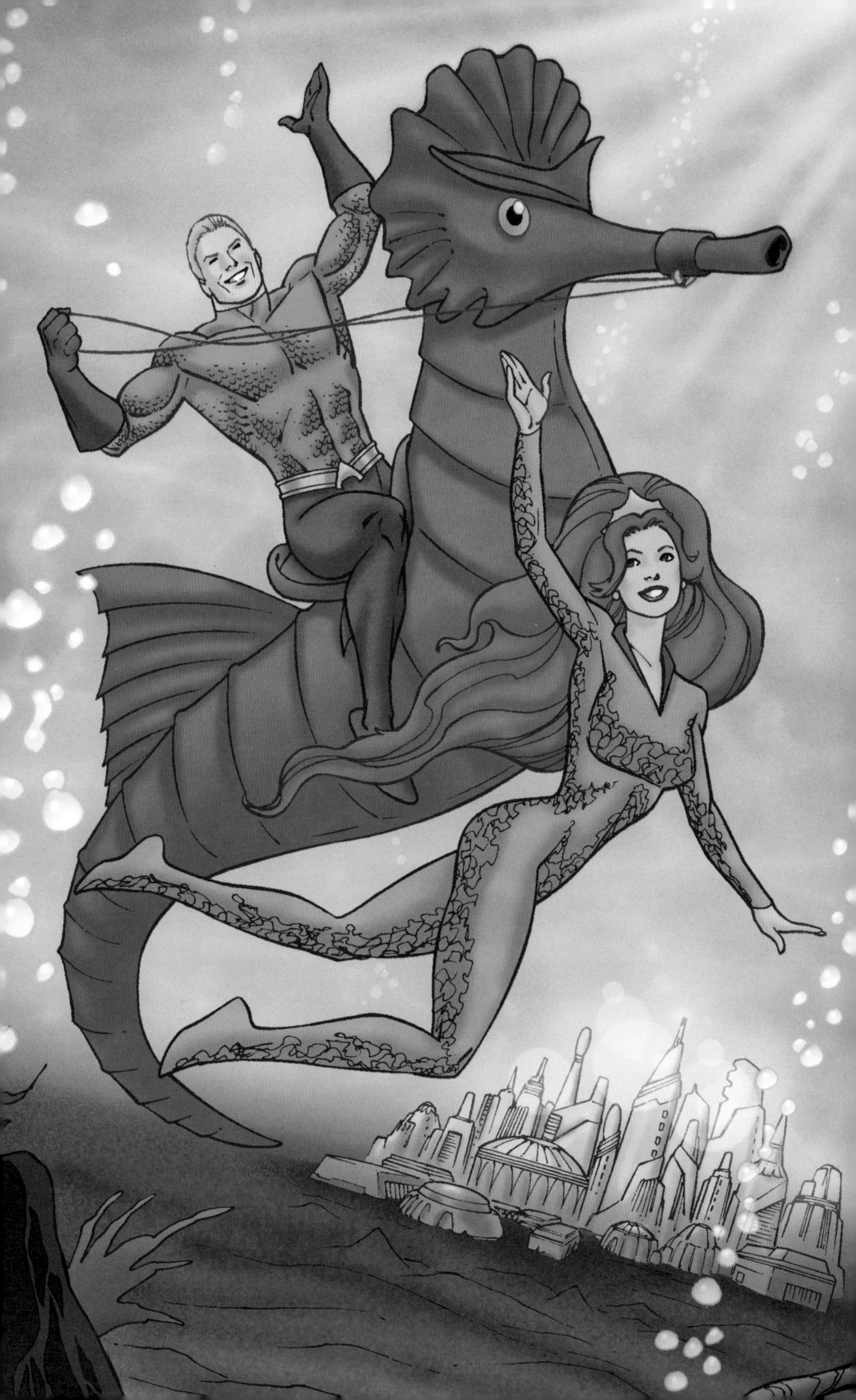

I am a member

of a team of super heroes

known as the Justice League!

The other heroes are coming

to Atlantis to meet Mera.

At the ocean's surface,

I greet Superman, Batman,

Wonder Woman, and Green Lantern

with giant seahorses for them to ride!

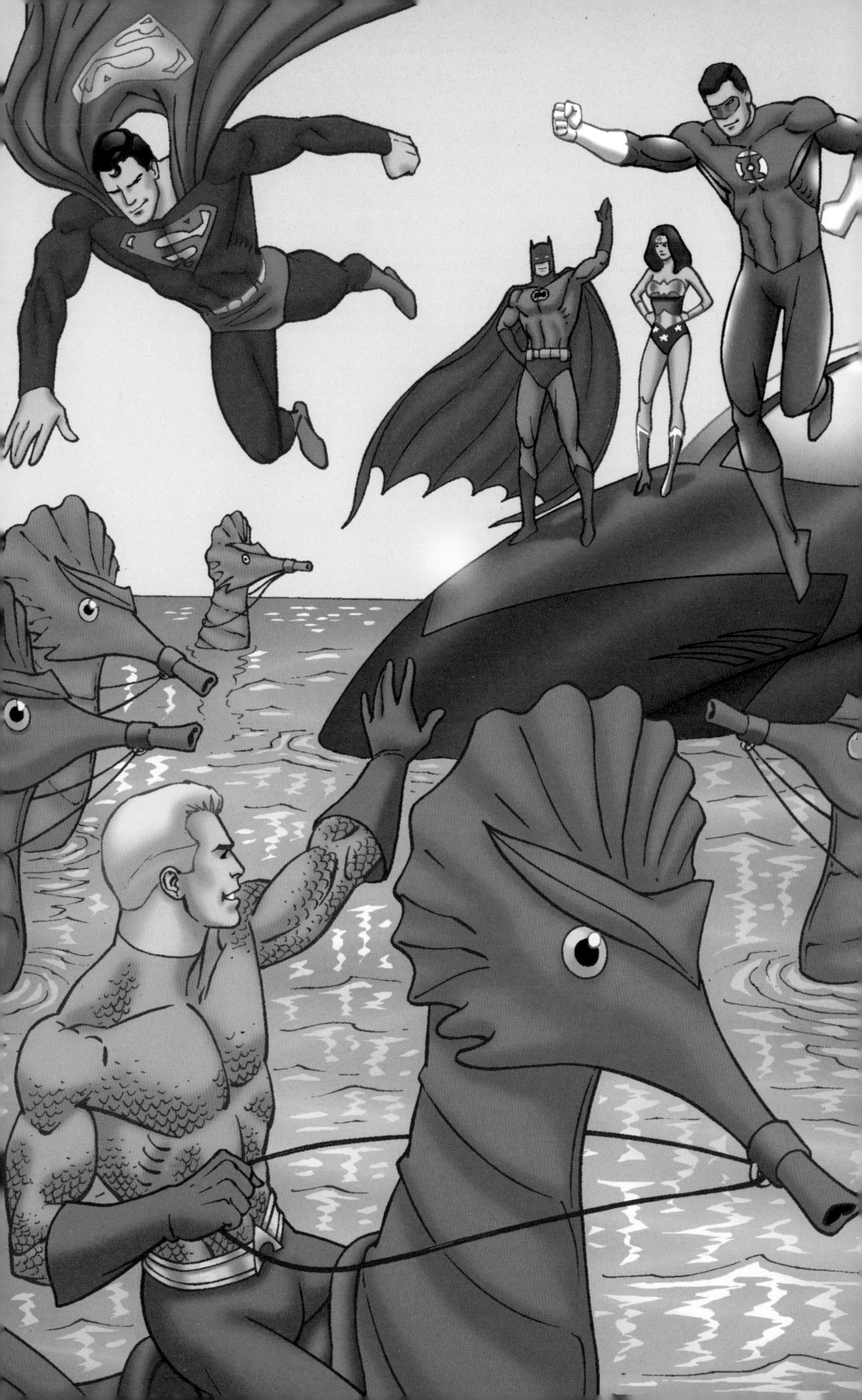

Wonder Woman and Superman
cannot wait to meet the Queen
of Atlantis!

Batman wants to see
my underwater castle.
I am excited to share
my world with my friends!

I can breathe underwater,

and Superman can hold his breath.

But Green Lantern must use his

power ring to create masks for the

other heroes so they can breathe.

After hopping onto our seahorses,

we head down to Atlantis.

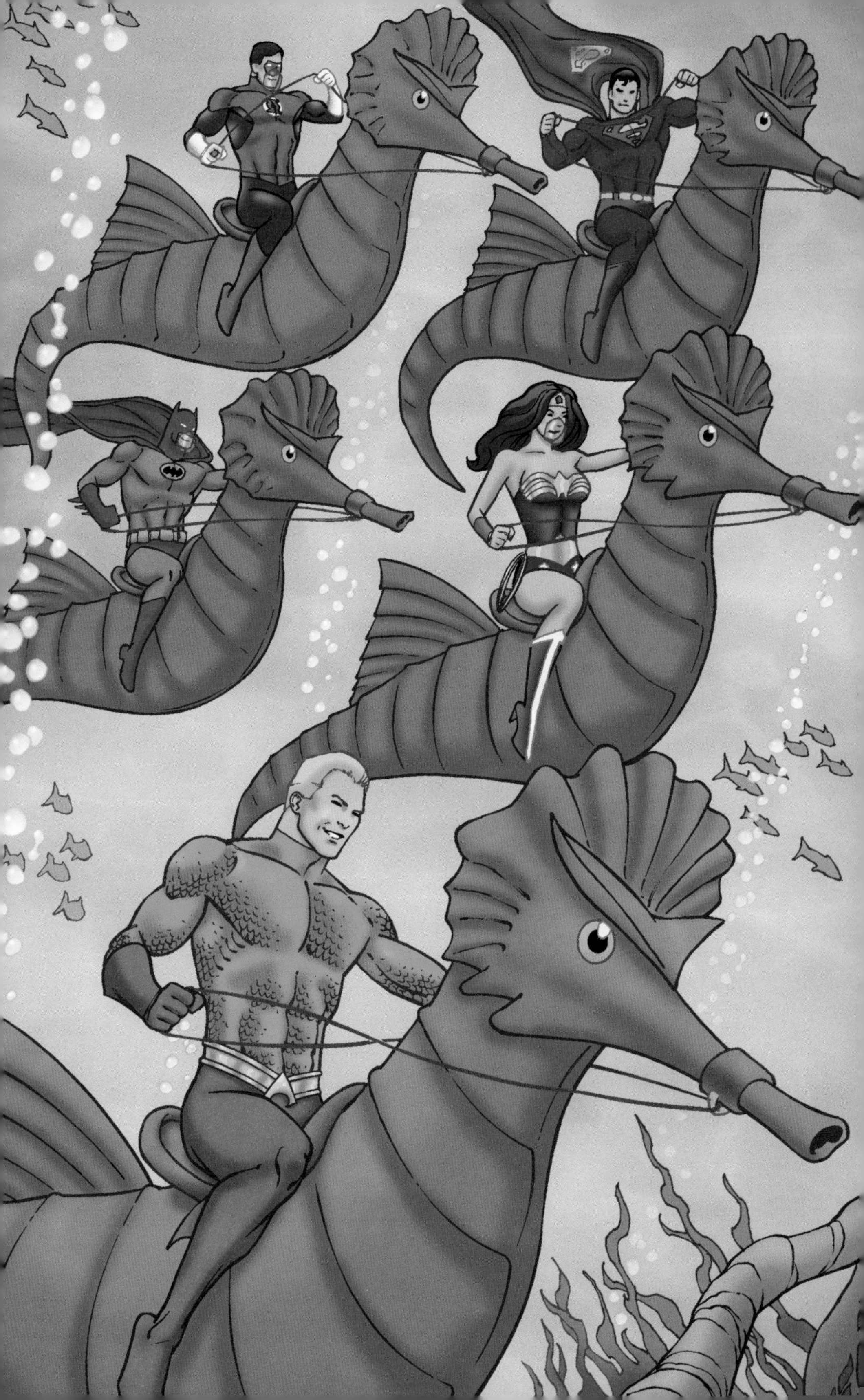

Before long, we arrive
at the golden castle.
I have something special
to show my friends.

Everyone meets Topo,
my pet octopus!
Topo likes to swim and
play in the throne room.

I lead my friends
into the royal dining room.
It is filled with air, so they
take off their masks.

Mera greets my friends
with a smile.
They are excited to taste
the delicious food!

Topo swims out to play
with his friends.
Suddenly, a submarine appears.
It has slipped through
Atlantis's defenses.

It belongs to Black Manta.

He is one of my greatest enemies!

I receive a message from
Topo's fish friends.
Atlantis is under attack!

Superman wants to help
us defend our city.

The rest of my friends jump
to their feet. They are ready
for anything!
We fearlessly face the enemy.

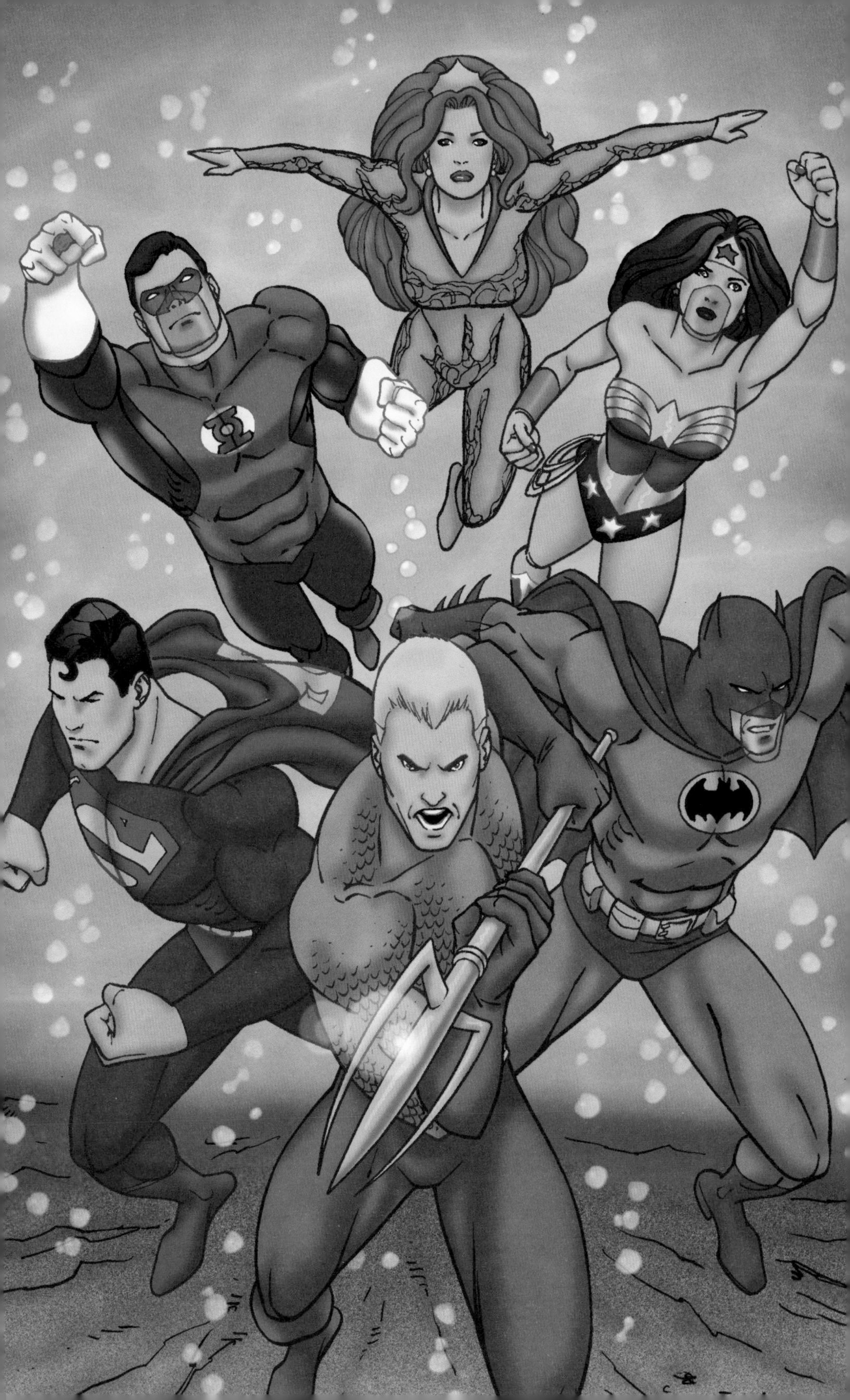

We soon spot Black Manta.

The villain swims out of his ship

wearing a diving suit and helmet.

But he is not alone!

King Shark is by his side.

He has brought an army

of sharks with them.

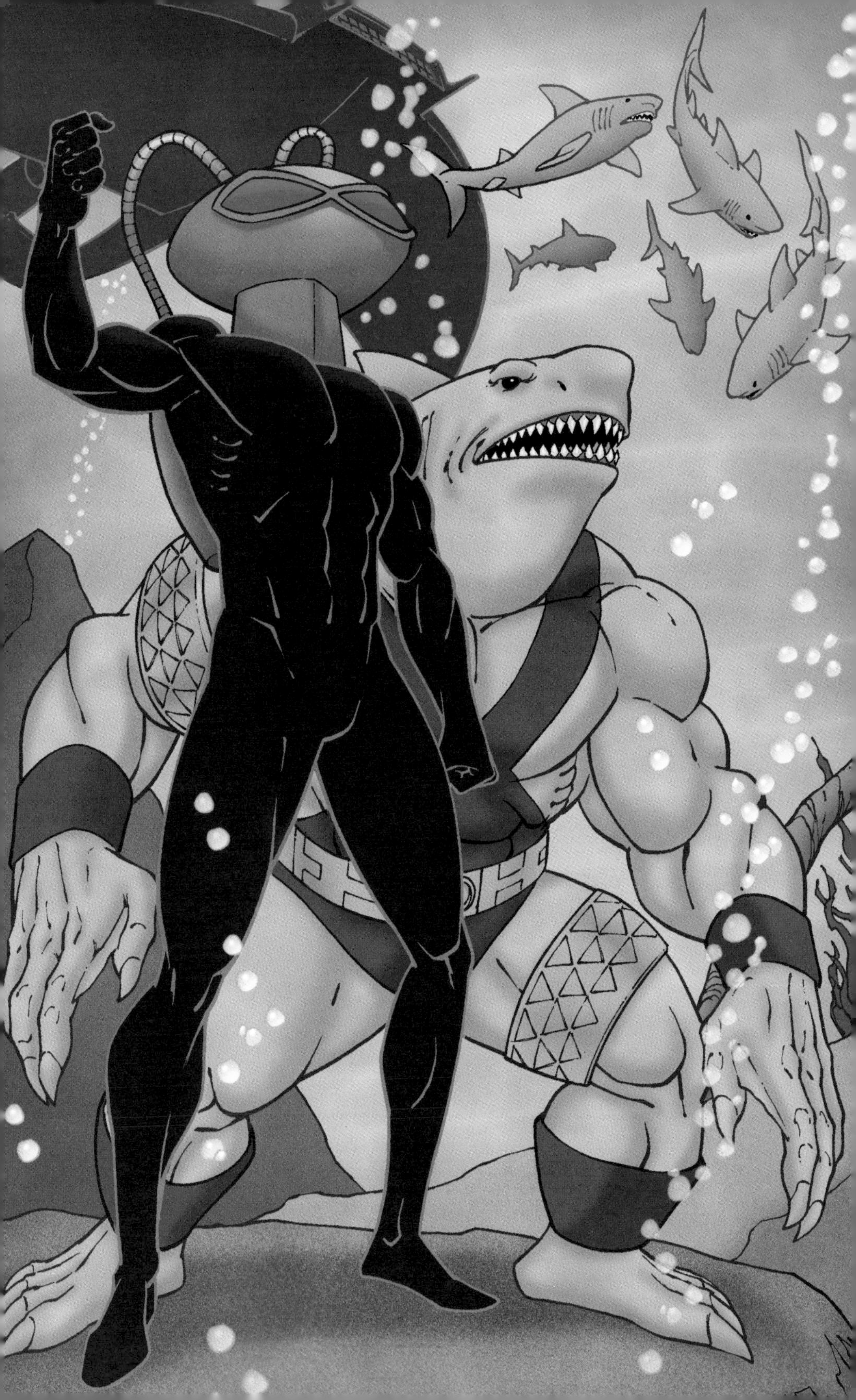

Green Lantern uses his
power ring to create
a big fishing net.
Queen Mera has powers, too!

She uses water to push the angry

sharks toward Green Lantern

so he can close the net!

King Shark tries to bite Superman
with his big sharp teeth.

Superman uses a powerful punch
to defeat the villain!

Black Manta fires

lasers from his helmet.

Wonder Woman deflects the rays

with her silver bracelets.

I join the fight with my

mighty trident!

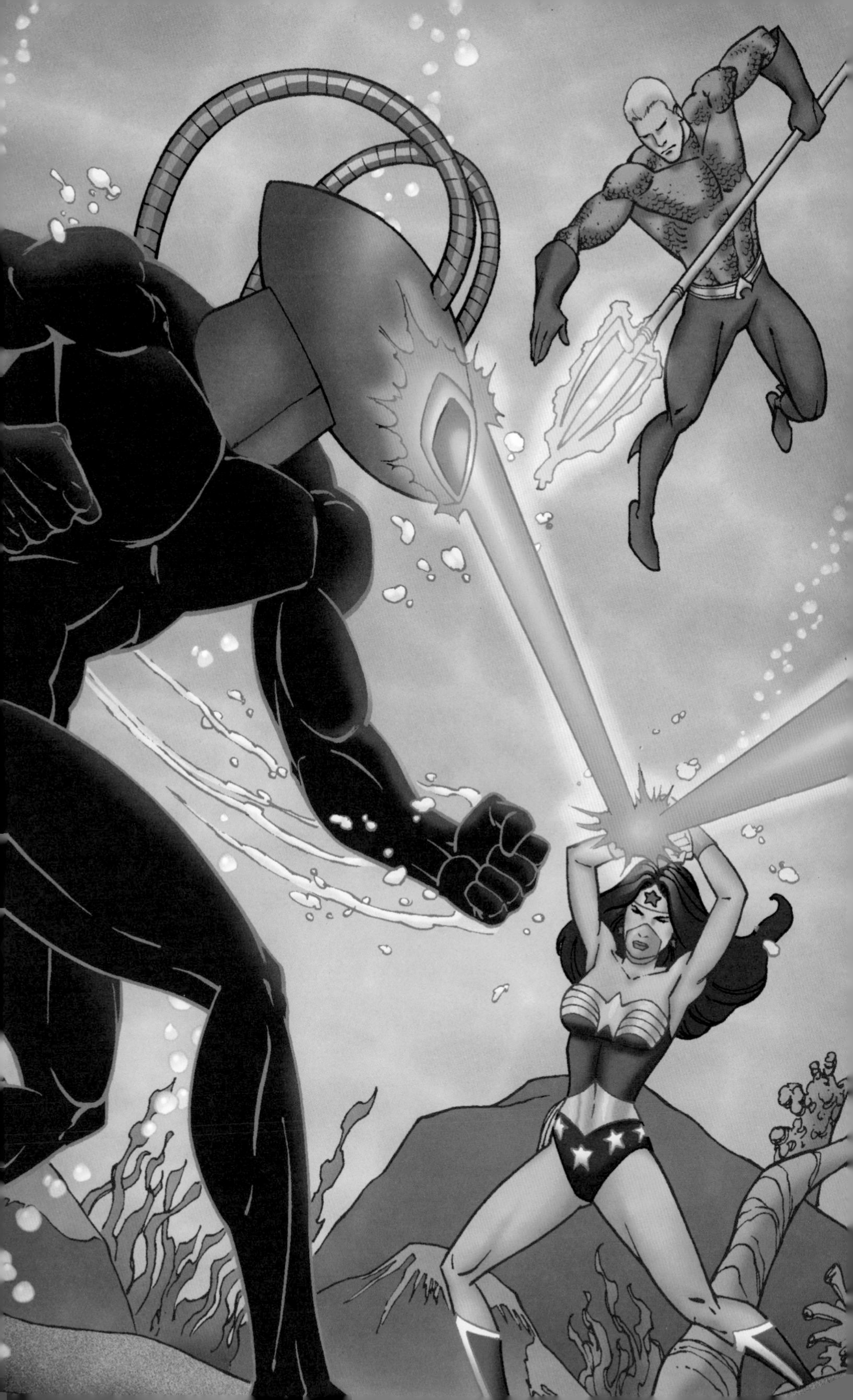

With the help of my friends,

Black Manta and King Shark

are quickly defeated.

We toss them into their ship.

Then I form a whirlpool

to send them far away.

My friends cheer.

Atlantis is safe once again!

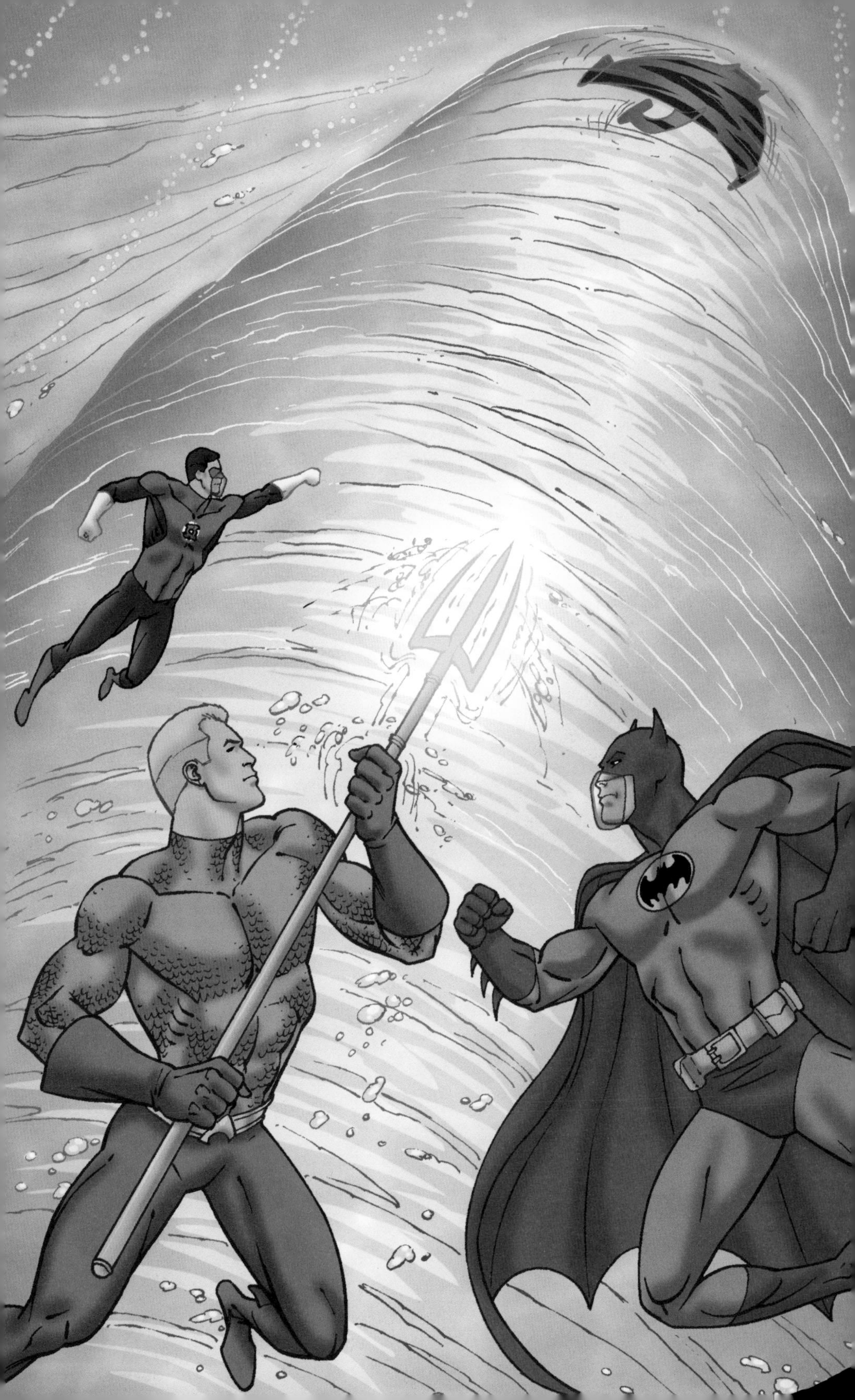

With help from my friends,

I am victorious.

I am King of the Seven Seas.

I am Aquaman!

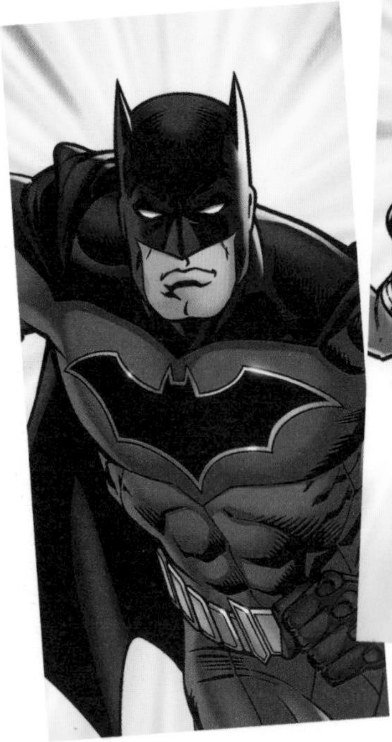
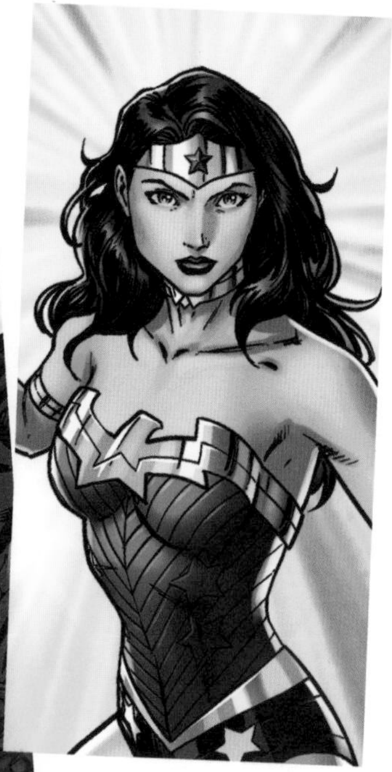

JUSTICE LEAGUE™

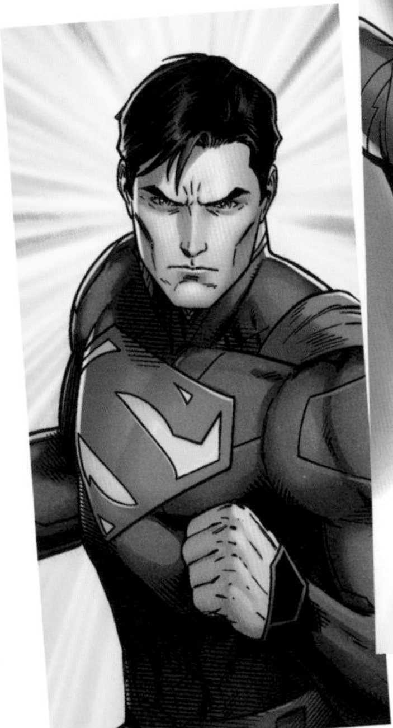

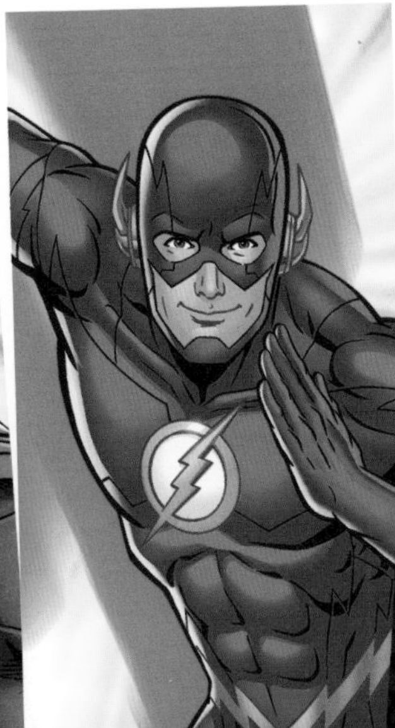

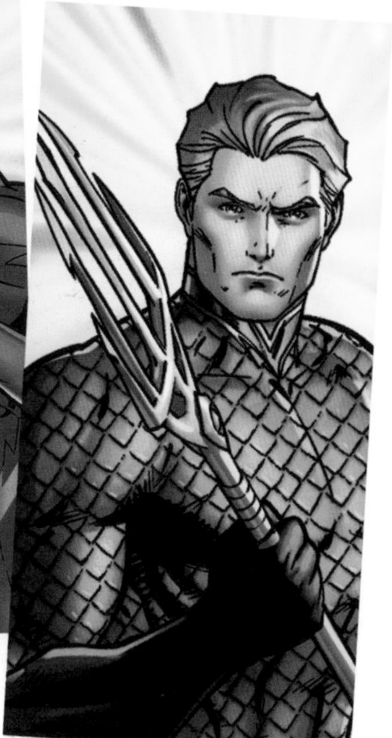

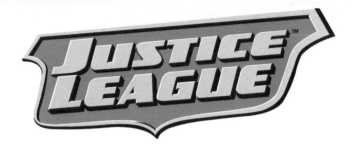